WINNER OF THE NEW WELSH WRITING AWARDS 2016

Bush Meat

New Welsh Rarebyte is the book imprint of New Welsh Review Ltd,
PO Box 170, Aberystwyth, Wales, SY23 1WZ,
www.newwelshreview.com, @newwelshreview,
Facebook.com/newelshreview
ISBN: 978-1-9997700-1-3

This work is available in ebook format through
White Glove publishing platform
Editor: Gwen Davies
With thanks to Samuel L Jones

Design & typesetting: Ingleby Davies Design
Printed and bound in Europe by Pulsio.
New Welsh Review Ltd works with the financial support of the
Welsh Books Council & Aberystwyth University

Bush Meat

Mandy Sutter

NEW
WELSH RAREBYTE

Also by Mandy Sutter

Permission to Stare, Slow Dancer Press, 1994
Game, Smith/Doorstop Books, 1995
Are You She (with Sidura Ludwig, Polly Wright & Myra Connell),
ed Lesley Glaister, Tindal Street Press, 2004
Travelling with the Bedouin Women of Hawd
(with Amina Souleiman), MAMA 2007
The Asylum Seeker (with Amina Souleiman), MAMA 2007
Stretching It, Indigo Dreams Publishing, 2013
Old Blue Car, Kettlebell Press, 2015

For my father

For my father

Bush Meat

Day after day, a boy tends his cows and watches the sky. The grass is brown; the animals dying; the trees unable to put forth leaves. The clouds cast shadows but release no rain. One day, an eagle flies overhead and a feather floats to the ground. The boy makes an arrow from the feather and shoots it into the dark clouds. The rain falls in sheets.

Under the wrecked frangipani bush, the bird sits like a steamboat. It's a Barbary duck, I think, with that strange red head that looks melted, as if a new face has run down and set on top of the old one.

'Is it an orphan?' asks Sarah.

'Don't go too close,' I say. 'Careful of your dress.'

The rain has pelted down all morning, making the red dirt shine. The locals will be glad: the dry season lasted forever apparently and killed half their livestock.

The bird makes a whirring sound.

'It's wagging its tail,' says Sarah.

At the bottom of the compound Chidike comes out of his hut, wearing the regulation red check shirt that the oil company provides for everyone's servants.

'It's time for your nap,' I tell Sarah.

But she waves him over. She was wary of him for the first few months then something changed. 'Look, Chidike! Look what I found!'

He looks at me. 'Madame.'

He can inject contempt into a single word. He crouches by the bush, in the litter of white wax petals. 'This bird, she swim down from Heaven. All the way.'

Sarah gazes at him.

He touches the bird. It shifts uneasily. 'Lucky for she, land at house with good, kind daughter.' I sigh. 'We dry her feather,' says Chidike.

Sarah reaches for the duck. I grab her wrist. 'I've told you about touching animals.'

'But *he* touched it!'

'That's different,' I say, glancing at him. But I know he'll never be on my side.

While Sarah is in her room, Chidike digs a hole behind the house. Jim gives him one of the thick pink plastic bags they use to keep the dynamite dry and by the time she comes out, Chidike has anchored it with stones and fitted the hosepipe to the outside tap. He and Sarah stand together, watching water trickle into the new pond.

When she finally comes in, she's covered in mud. I can't help gasping. I spent hours on the sewing machine making that dress. The fabric here is wonderful, so gaily patterned, even if the dye does run.

'Don't fuss,' says Jim. 'We're not in Tuffley Avenue now.'

I nod. I was a teacher back in England. Letting things drop is my main job here.

The duck isn't the only thing the rains bring. The next day when

I'm making dinner, the insect mesh on the back door rattles.

'Hello. Hello.' It's a pleasant voice. Still I shout for Chidike, who's meant to field callers. I go on fiddling with the oven. It's a Creda Simplex, all the rage here but I haven't seen one in England for years. The temperature knob's so basic. Baking is hit and miss. Of course, Chidike doesn't come. 'Hello,' I hear again. 'Hello, madame.'

The voice is like wind chimes. I open the door to a man in sagging khaki shorts. He is barefoot and bony, his skin the colour of damsons.

He shuffles from foot to foot. '*Aha mu bu* Michael.' I don't know what to do. The rules are different here. You try and pick things up from the other wives, but your mistakes are one of their main sources of entertainment. The man draws a wilted paper from his shorts pocket. It says Nigeria Hotel and Catering School. 'Certificate!' he says, and pushes it at me.

I step back. This is how they get you, the wives say. They make you take something and then before you know it, they've moved all their women, children, uncles, goats, chickens and monkeys into your servants' block.

'I have nothing for you,' I say. He beams. 'I said no vacancies!' I speak extra clearly, Queen's English. An awful lot of things from school come back to you here, things you thought were useless. 'I already have help in the house.'

That isn't strictly true. But one day Chidike will learn to take instructions from a woman.

The man frowns. 'No, madame. Not houseboy. I chef. I measure tea*spoon*, table*spoon*. I bake macaroni cheese. Fish in white sauce.'

The leather thong around his neck looks as if it has been

there always. Next to it he wears a silver cross on a chain.

We can't afford two servants. I'd rather have none, but it isn't up to me.

'I'm sure you are very skilled. But I'm not looking for a chef.'

'Yes, skilled,' he says. 'Looking for. Roast beef, Yorkshire pudding. I bake boiled egg. I bake vanilla ice cream. I am read British cookbook, follow recipe.'

Behind him by the pond, the duck rummages under its wing. It's cleaner already, a cloud come down to earth.

I glance at his ribs, his collarbone. Not an ounce or even a tablespoon of spare flesh on him.

His feet are cracked. 'Yes,' he says, as if I've asked him a question. 'I from Owerri side.' He points at the hills. They are red today. Sometimes they are purple. Owerri is thirty miles distant. Has he walked all the way?

'What's your real name?' I ask. '*Kedu aha gi*?' That's Igbo I think.

'*Aha mu bu Michael.* My name Michael.'

'Yes. And your Nigerian name?' He frowns. 'Are you Igbo, Michael? Yoruba?'

There are other tribes in the Delta but I can't remember their names. He looks away. Perhaps it's a rude question.

He pulls something else out. It's a Polaroid photo, of an old woman standing in front of a hut. She has his skin and wears a wrap patterned with orange sunflowers. Her arms are sticks; the fabric is clean and bright. Five children stand about her, three items of clothing between them. A man's shirt comes down the ankles of a small boy.

'Are these your children?' I ask. 'Your mother?'

He frowns. He doesn't seem to like questions.

'Your family, perhaps,' I say.

'Family, yes.'

I wonder where his wife is. And suddenly I am holding the photo and he is grinning.

I can see the wives saying I'm weak; have fallen for a trick. I can hear the relish in their voices as they pass the story round.

But I hear myself asking if he wants a glass of water. He looks worried. 'You are thirsty, perhaps,' I say.

'Thirsty, yes.'

Jim stands in the kitchen doorway, nursing his glass. The whisky goes further up the sides every day. 'The trouble with this country is the black man thinks he owns it.' I thought he did own it, but I say nothing, just tip the last of the Fray Bentos steak and kidney pies from the pan where it has been boiling and wonder if they'll ever get more in at Kingsway. Even frozen chicken is getting scarce. 'The sooner he grasps the notion that land can be bought and sold, the better off he'll be,' says Jim.

Out of the window, Sarah claps at the duck. She's been out there all afternoon training it. There's nothing wrong with that, I suppose. But how long will the duck stick around? I don't want her getting attached.

I begin opening the pie tin. The gravy is solid.

'I mean, it's endemic,' says Jim. 'I found some vagrant in our back garden earlier.' I frown. I told Michael I'd ask at the British Club; that it would take a day or two. But he sat down with his back against the side wall, immediately comfortable as though waiting was something he understood. 'Got rid of him, of course,' says Jim. 'Told him this was private property. I mean, when will they grasp it?' Ice clicks against his teeth.

I wonder what will happen if Jim finds new sources of oil. I wonder what will happen if he doesn't. I glance at the cupboard. Inside, the photo and certificate stand between bags of flour. No-one looks in there but me. A proper oil company wife would have thrown them out by now, assuming they were fakes, which they probably are. If she'd ever accepted them in the first place. I slide the pie onto a plate. 'I told him there was a rifle in the house and I wouldn't hesitate to use it,' says Jim.

'A rifle?'

Jim waves his whisky. 'Calm down. It's not technically here. It's down the road, at the Williams place. But that's not the point. This bloke was making himself at home on our land. Well, our rented land. Was he bothering you? You should have called me.'

'He wasn't bothering me. I gave him a glass of water, that's all.'

'You did what?' I take the peas off the heat. 'You realise you'll never get rid of him now?' says Jim. 'You realise word will go round on the bush telegraph and we'll have every good-for-nothing in the Delta knocking on our door?'

'Oh, surely not,' I say. 'Give Sarah a call, will you? Tell her to come in and wash her hands.'

It's getting late, and night comes suddenly here. 'Please. The dinner will go cold.'

Jim grunts and goes out. Cooking, sewing, the needs of growing children: all these things are outside his ken.

When I open the back door next morning, Michael is there again, leaning against the wall. I assume he's wearing different shorts, until I see they are yesterday's, wet through.

'Hello. Hello,' he sings, his teeth chattering.

'Have you been waiting there all night?'

'I sit under left eye of God.'

'But you're soaked to the skin.'

'Thunder is happy gift, bring much life.'

I don't know what to say so I go down the compound with the teapot. He follows. The duck is by the generator. It likes the generator, which is warm and has a heartbeat of sorts.

I throw the tea leaves on the compost heap. 'What for Madame heap him rabis?' asks Michael.

'It's not really rubbish. It's vegetable peelings and eggshells and tea leaves. Natural materials. They'll break down then I'll use them to feed the garden.' He nods. I don't think he's understood. There's a spade by the compost heap and I dig it in. The stuff at the base is already black. It's always a shock, how quickly natural processes happen out here. How quickly things grow; how quickly they die. 'It's food for the plants,' I say. 'Don't you make compost in your village?'

He frowns. I try again. 'You grow vegetables in your village, perhaps.'

'In my village, grow cassava, grow yam, make good cargo for market.'

'Well, if you spread compost, your yams grow bigger.'

I hold my hands around the fat girth of an imaginary yam.

He looks blank. I take a spade full of compost and lead him to my broken frangipani. I spread it around the bottom of the bush, and pat it down.

'Ah, for help him greens!' says Michael. 'For help him flower. I like him true.'

That evening while I'm laying the table, I tell Jim I'll take the money out of my housekeeping.

Jim's tumbler sounds on the glass topped table. 'You've discussed wages with him?'

I place napkins alongside table mats. 'Only in theory. I've thought about his board, too. He can sleep in the hut with Chidike.'

Jim goes to the drinks cabinet. Gordons, Captain Morgan, Famous Grouse, Campari, Warninks: a rainbow of bottles that the crew bring in from Fernando Po. They cost next to nothing. He pours himself another whisky.

'He only wants one day off a month,' I say. 'He showed me a photo of his family. Jim, they do look poor. I think his wife's dead.'

'You can't go around putting people on our payroll just because they look poor.'

'A shilling a week is very reasonable for a trained chef.'

'But what if Chidike doesn't want to share? For one thing, this Michael character is probably from a different tribe.'

I wonder why Chidike's preferences matter. 'The hut's big enough for two families, let alone two men.'

'But I thought you wanted to keep house yourself. You said you were looking forward to it, as a change from going out to work.'

It's true, I did say that. But I suppose one says a lot of things.

The first dish Michael serves is chicken, a frozen one I've managed to get at Kingsway. He bears it in on a chopping board and sets it in front of Jim. He's covered it with my cut-glass bowl. Over his shorts and a red check shirt, he wears my apron with the yellow daisies. It's too big for him, but then most clothes are.

'What's he doing with the trifle dish?' shrieks Sarah.

'Don't talk about Michael as though he isn't here,' I say.

Our carving set, a wedding present from seven years ago, lives in a blue velvet-lined box. Jim strafes the knife on the sharpener.

Michael lifts the bowl.

Smoke billows out.

'Cockerel,' says Michael. 'I been cook him long.'

'A tad too long, by the looks of things,' says Jim, as the smoke clears.

'It is a little overdone on top,' I say. 'I'm sure it'll be all right in the middle.'

Michael beams.

Jim digs the fork in. Black flakes drop off. 'Piercing through the igneous strata,' he says and lays a slice of meat on the board. 'Arriving at the molten core.' The slice is pink in the middle, and glitters with ice. Red water leaks into the grooves of the board. Jim brings out a plastic bag on the end of the fork. 'He's left the giblets in!'

Sarah's laugh is almost a scream.

It begins to dawn on Michael that all is not well. 'Chop no good?'

'Chop no good,' I say. 'But oven finish. Oven *bosaut*, understand?'

'That's the first I've heard of it,' says Jim.

In the kitchen, Chidike leans by the back door.

'Why didn't you show Michael how to use the cooker?' I ask.

Chidike looks amused. 'Michael is train cook, Madame. I am house boy only.'

9

Michael is lurking by the sink. 'Are there any vegetables?' I ask him. He chews his lip. 'You have, perhaps, boiled some vegetables,' I say. 'Potatoes, greens.'

'I boil, yes.'

'Well, let's have a look at them. Bring them in.'

'This bloke's a bit of a joke, isn't he?' says Jim when I go back in.

'He might have one or two things to learn. But he'll pick up. It's a question of explaining things in a way he can understand.'

Michael comes back in and puts a cake tin on the table, full of boiled potatoes and carrots. Then come three teacups, with green stew inside.

'Are we supposed to eat it or drink it?' grumbles Sarah.

'Whatever you like, dear,' I say.

The stew is glutinous but tastes good.

'This is lovely, Michael,' I say. 'It is perhaps spinach.'

'Na spinach, madame. *Soko*. *Soko*.' Saying a word in his own language seems to calm him. 'Is call *soko*,' he says again.

'Why are you being so nice to that man?' Sarah wants to know when I'm tucking her into her mosquito net.

'I don't know about nice.'

'You *are*.' She works her Sindy doll's hair.

'Well, why shouldn't we be nice to the people here? They're letting us stay in their country.'

The sound of the cicadas swells and falls like the sea.

'We should be grateful to Michael, especially,' I add. 'He's left his family to help us.'

The doll, in its British Airways outfit, is getting cornrow plaits.

'Chidike calls him Bones-das-all,' says Sarah. 'He's a bush man, you see.'

'Oh. And what's a bush man, when he's at home?'

'Someone who can't read or write,' she says. 'I think.'

I finish tucking her in. 'Did Chidike say it in a nasty way?'

'He just said it.'

'To Michael, or to you?'

'Will Chidike get into trouble with Daddy, now?'

'Chidike and Michael are friends, Sarah. Like you and Omo, at school. Chidike lent Michael a shirt.'

'He didn't lend it him, he sold it him,' says Sarah. 'But he won't get his money till pay day.'

I stare at her. 'What makes you say that?'

She shrugs and begins another plait. '*I* don't know. Mummy, next time we go to Port Harcourt, can we buy Adaku some cracked corn? Chidike says it's what she likes to eat best.'

'Who's Adaku?'

'Adaku the *duck*.'

At seven the next morning, Michael's already in the kitchen and steam rolls in bolsters across the ceiling. He's making tea in a saucepan.

I go over and take the pan off the heat. 'I can make our tea in the mornings.'

He clutches the black and gold caddy, with its faded picture of Tower Bridge. 'But, is pleasure make tea for Madame. When oven is bugger up, Madame is then good friend to Michael.'

'Okay. But have your own breakfast first. Make your own tea, down in the hut.'

He drops his gaze. 'If Madame wish it.'

'But you don't, perhaps.'

He looks at his feet. 'If Madame wish, then Michael wish.'

'Things are not comfortable in the hut, perhaps.'

'Certainly Madame, is comfortable. Is only, what I go do down there?'

'Alright,' I say.

The pan is full of swollen tea leaves. I wonder if I can dry them out and reuse them.

Michael studies my face. 'Because why this tea is bad?'

'It's not bad, Michael. But Madame likes her tea so-so.'

I put the kettle on and get the teapot out.

'*Chei!*' says Michael. 'What is this?' I swill hot water around the pot. 'This pot belong tea,' says Michael.

'Yes. It's what we use in England. It makes the tea leaves go further. We only put in one spoonful for each person who wants a cup of tea, plus one for the pot. You'll find the spoon in the tin.'

'Cap tea,' he says, fishing the spoon out of the caddy. 'Understand.'

'So, if there are two people who want tea, you would use three spoonfuls.'

'One for person, one for pot.'

I put the warmed pot down. 'If Master and Madame both want tea, how many spoonfuls should you put in?' He nods, but doesn't speak. 'Master, madame,' I say. 'Sarah doesn't like tea.'

'How many are these persons?' he asks.

I hold up two fingers. With the utmost care he transfers two spoonfuls of tea into the pot. 'One for the person,' I say. 'And one for...'

'One for pot,' he says. 'Understand.'

He puts another spoonful in. But then he goes to add a second.

'No, only one for the pot,' I say, holding up one finger.

He stands thinking. 'One for pot, no matter how many are the persons?'

'Exactly.'

He looks delighted. 'Yes, sir! Now I straight.'

I can't help laughing.

Early next morning, while Jim is trying not to wake up, there's a tap at the bedroom door.

'Just a minute,' I call, pulling the sheet quickly about me.

I hear the rattle of a tray. 'I lose him tea here.'

'Thank you, Michael. Very good!'

'That's my eardrum you're shattering,' mutters Jim.

The tea, when I pour it, glows clear amber in the white cup.

Tea is one thing, though. I'm obviously going to have to teach Michael to cook.

Over the next few days, I show him how to make macaroni cheese, poached eggs on toast, corned beef pie. His skills or lack of them are hard to predict. He struggles to heat milk and grate cheese, but he knows how to make pastry.

'You have a light touch,' I say.

'Thank you Madame. Make pastry, same as make *chin-chin*.'

'*Chin-chin*?'

'Bush cake. But, British cake better.'

'Still, you must show me how to make it.'

'If Madame wish it.'

He approves of the rolling pin. 'Hand and stone, them reign pass,' he says.

The corned beef he's not keen on. He watches as the key turns and a stripe of mottled pink meat appears.

'Madame eat this grease?' he asks as the block slides out,

yellow crusted, onto the chopping board.

'It all goes in,' I say, cubing the meat and scraping it into a pan with chopped carrots and onions. The pie filling begins to bubble, pinkly.

'This is British recipe for pie?' he asks, doubtful.

'We use proper meat if we have it. Steak and kidney. Chicken, lamb... but never mind. We have a special sauce. It covers a multitude of sins.'

I open the fridge to show him the bottle of HP.

As I glance at the familiar blue label with its smudged picture of the Houses of Parliament, a yearning for home sweeps me up without warning. I stand there in the cool of the open fridge, blinking back tears. I cover my mouth. I dread a question, about the name, about the picture. But Michael stands looking at the floor and barely breathing, as if the slightest move or sound would be an insult.

When I've recovered and we've begun peeling potatoes again, he asks, 'Madame not know for meat man store?'

'Yes. We go to Kingsway. In Port Harcourt.'

'Kingsway no,' says Michael. 'Meat man store Ikot Ekpene Road. Is close to, Madame. Few metre long.'

'Really?'

The wives haven't mentioned a butcher's shop. And I can't remember seeing any shops on the Ikot Ekpene Road, which is long and charmless and makes you feel as if you're going from nowhere to nowhere.

'Meat man sell cow leg,' says Michael. 'Meat man son my fadda broda.'

'He's your cousin.'

'Cousin, yes.'

The corned beef filling is already mush.

'But all the cows are dead, Michael,' I say. 'Aren't they?'

It's safe enough in our area, probably. You hear things about violent robberies, about white people being targets. But there's no local radio or paper to back up the stories. The BBC World Service is all we have, broadcasting from another planet. Once, on the way back from school, three boys danced out of nowhere and surrounded Sarah. One tugged her hair, and she shrieked and threw her arms up. Then the boys were gone and so was her bracelet, the one her Nana had bought silver charms for since the day she was born.

Sarah wasn't upset at the time, just gazed at her bare wrist and let it float up in front of her face. I cried with the shock and the feeling I should have been able to stop it. But perhaps it did affect her. Now at lunch, when I suggest a trip to the butchers, she doesn't want to go.

'You have to,' I say. 'Your father is going back to work and I'm not leaving you here alone.'

Sarah stops eating. 'I won't be on my own. Chidike will be here. And Adaku.'

'Who?' asks Jim.

'The duck,' I say. 'Chidike's name for it, apparently. Means Born Into Wealth. Adaku isn't a good babysitter,' I tell Sarah. 'And Chidike has work to do.'

'Adaku *is* good!' says Sarah. 'She's a spirit come up from the waters beneath the earth to watch over me and keep me safe.'

Jim snorts.

'Safe from who?' I ask. Sarah looks uncertain. 'I can't see a duck, even one as fierce as Adaku, being much use if you were really in danger.' I say.

'She's not really a *duck*. She's an ancestor who's taken on duck form.'

'Why would Grandad want to come back as a duck?' I ask. 'He wouldn't be able to smoke his pipe.'

Jim laughs and Sarah shoots me a look of disgust.

Along the Ikot Ekpene Road, the houses are sparse; the sun bores down; monkeys scream as we pass. Everyone has monkeys out here but you can't see them as pets. Even Sarah can't, and she can make a pet out of anything.

Michael leads the way, his tread light on the road. Up ahead, three young women walk home from market. Their bodies swing beneath their loads: a large white bowl, a bale of blue cloth, a Singer sewing machine. They talk with their hands, keep their heads level.

I hold onto Sarah in case more boys wait their chance to surround her. Our hands make a slippery knot.

After half an hour of walking, Michael stops outside a bungalow that was once white, with a roof made of rust. 'Meat man store!' he announces.

There's no sign and nothing to mark it out from the next house a hundred yards away. Michael heads down a side path. Sarah twists in my grip.

We hear the clamour of the generator before we see it, hunkered under two broken umbrellas. Next to it stands a low concrete hut. An old man nods to us from a stool and pokes a broken polystyrene tile into the tangle of flies above his head.

Michael parts the bead curtain that hangs in the doorway and beckons us through.

Inside it's dark and cool. Slowly, the room makes itself visible. A counter runs its width, two chest freezers behind it. A

Fly-o-cutor glows violet. The man behind the counter, who seems to be wearing a woman's mac, shakes hands with Michael then bows. At one end of the counter stands a circular saw, its teeth gummed with pink paste.

'Welcome, madame. You are well?'

'Yes, thank you.'

'Your family they are well?'

'Very well. Your family also?'

'Old fadda, him take breeze,' says the man, nodding towards the door.

You can talk like this all day if you want to.

'My cook tells me you have beef for sale.'

'Beef, no. Bush meat. I have bush meat.'

I glance at Michael. I don't know what bush meat is, but he seems undisturbed by the news.

'Well, let's see it.' Having come all the way here, I might as well.

The man opens a freezer, which lets out a narcotic puff of cold air, and hoists a translucent lump onto the counter. It has many planes, as if pieces have been sawn off any old how.

I sense limbs and bodies packed together beneath the glassy surface like bottled fruit. My hope of a succulent, chunky casserole, one I can boast about to the other wives, withers and dies.

'You want big piece?' asks the meat-man.

'What sort of meat is it, exactly?'

'Bush meat.' He hefts the frozen trapezoid block onto the saw bed. I hesitate. A pink puddle begins to form on the counter.

'How much you want, madame?'

Above, a fly roasts with a snap and a fizz. Sarah stands by the strings of light in the doorway. Michael has lost his smile.

'Okay,' I say. 'Small piece only.'

The meat-man reaches down to a switch under the counter. He introduces the rose block to the blurred edge and a sibilant grating begins. Sarah's hands fly to her ears. I try not to think of the blade passing through chests, necks, tails.

The portion skates across the counter. The meat man turns the saw off but the air still rings. He slings the rest of the meat back into the freezer and produces a grubby plastic bag. Sarah starts to cry.

'Don't worry, love,' I whisper, 'we'll soon be home.'

'I won't eat it,' says Sarah. 'I won't and you can't make me.'

I stare at her.

'There are dogs' ears in there,' she says. 'I saw them.'

'Nah, nah,' says the meat-man. 'Nah make Bingo for chop, madame. For chop, make cow leg. For chop make bush pig, make grass cutter, make porcupine.'

'Take no notice,' I say, extracting coins from my purse. 'She's only a child. She misses her dog. We had to leave him behind in England.'

The beads on the curtain dance their goodbye. The light outside is dazzling. The old man sits, poking at flies.

'There are no dogs' ears, love,' I say.

She cries all the way home.

I decide to stew the meat with potatoes and onions; treat it like rabbit. It does look a bit like rabbit.

'Dis Missis Beeto,' says Michael. 'She good friend from Madame, live in London, England?'

'She lived a hundred years ago, Michael. But because she wrote her recipes down, we've still got them. Understand?'

'Yes, yes,' he says, impatient.

Sarah, a picky eater at the best of times, refuses to eat the stew. I don't force her.

'Christ, this meat's full of tiny bones,' says Jim. 'It's as bad as eating fish.'

Back in the kitchen, Michael scrapes waste food into the bin.

'Thank you for today,' I say. 'The meat made an excellent stew.'

He hands me the dirty plates. 'If Madame happy, then Michael happy.'

But he doesn't look happy. To distract him, I ask whether in his village they believe that dead people come back in the form of animals and birds. 'Chidike thinks our duck is an ancestor,' I smile.

Michael looks grave. 'Belief in bird spirit is ignorant belief, belief from bush man. In we village, belief in Fadda, Son and Holy goat. Belief in Jesu Christ and Wirgin Mary, Holy mudda from God.'

To save his reputation with my family, Michael needs to make something delicious. I decide on ice cream: Jim and Sarah love it, even the odd brick of Walls we sometimes find at Kingsway, misshapen as though it has melted and refrozen a few times.

I line eggs up on the worktop.

'*Chei*!' says Michael when I tell him how much they've cost, a price that makes me wonder if you can use duck eggs to make ice cream instead. If the duck ever lays any. If the duck is even female.

The whisking action is new to him and he has to rest his arm. We're both excited when the eggs and cream thicken over the pan of hot water. We pour the mixture into the two ice block trays.

Michael is uncertain. 'But Master drink whisky on top him rocks.'

'He won't mind, just this once.'

He doesn't. The ice cream, when it comes out of the freezer smoking, is as creamy and white as a frangipani flower.

'Good God,' he says, 'is that what I think it is?'

Michael's fingers stick to the metal trays, leaving balloon-shaped ovals.

The ice cream makes our mouths swim with cold sweetness.

Jim chuckles. 'Eating ice cream in the middle of the bush! Wait till the Party Manager hears about this.'

I notice that Sarah is mashing hers up with the back of her spoon. 'Have you tasted it, darling? It's lovely.'

'No.'

'Why not?'

Sarah eyes Michael. 'Because *he* made it. The coconut head.'

I can't get my breath. 'What a horrid thing to say.' Jim eats on. 'I won't stand for it, Sarah,' I say. 'Michael is part of our household and you will respect him accordingly.'

Jim pushes his bowl away. 'Nice drop of ice cream, whoever made it.'

'Eat it, Sarah,' I say, my face hot. 'All the work that's gone into it. I won't see it wasted.'

'May I get down from the table?' asks Sarah.

'No,' I say.

'Of course she can,' says Jim.

And she gets down, as self-composed as you like, and pushes her chair carefully in under the table.

I turn to Michael to reassure him it isn't his fault, that the ice cream is perfect. He's not there.

'Where's Michael?' I ask.

'God knows,' says Jim. 'But I'm off down to the Club.'

I sit with the abandoned dishes, fighting tears.

Chidike comes in and speaks gently. 'Michael done run, Madame. Him done thief my shirt.'

The next day, the household feels strange. We're a family with one servant too few, one too many. I expect swagger from Chidike, but he defeats me even in that, watering my frangipani and sweeping the stairs without once banging the broom against the skirting board.

Sarah sulks and seems preoccupied every time I speak. I don't try to mend things. I'm cross with her over Michael, even though it isn't really her fault. I'm cross with Jim, too. But he won't acknowledge my mood and by evening, I've given it up.

'Let's face it,' says Jim. 'He'd never have shaken down with Chidike. They might have put on a show of it for our sakes, but they hated each other's guts.'

I try to be comforted.

But as the week goes on, there's a space in my mornings where the cookery lessons were. And a sense that I've been wrong about the world. That it has shown itself to be a mean place, after all.

Chukwuma Three Shilling gets new fabric in at his market stall so I decide to concentrate on my sewing; make myself something for a change. I buy some lovely cotton in emerald green with white flowers. The dress takes a day. With an off cut, I make a trouser suit for Sarah's Sindy doll, a fiddly job which takes almost as long as the dress.

Then I apply myself to getting the oven fixed. The Party Manager has a friend who worked for the Electricity Board in Nottingham and he comes round one morning. He turns the oven on and off a few times, opens the door and gets down on his knees, shirt buttons straining. He's still there three hours later. I offer him a coffee but he wants beer. The thermostat's a sod, pardon his French. I deserve a new cooker, a pretty young housewife like me, catering for a hungry family on the edge of the bloody jungle. When he leaves, I feel exhausted.

The insect mesh rattles and my heart sinks. I glance around the floor for a lost screwdriver.

But it isn't the Party Manager's friend. 'Madame. *Kedu*!'

Michael stands at the kitchen door, a massive yam in each hand. 'Present from we village *Iso koko*: tip top quality wegetable!'

He looks the same as when he left, feet and shorts filthy but red check shirt pristine. I nearly throw my arms around him.

I manage to stop myself. 'Come in, Michael. It's good to see you back. But we need to talk.' I put the yams on the draining board and sit at the breakfast bar. I know better than to ask him to sit. Chidike always leans on the door with his arms folded but Michael stands upright with his hands at his sides, like a soldier. 'Going off the way you did was unacceptable. If you are to work for me, I must be able to rely on you.' I pause for effect. 'You've been back to your village. There, perhaps you found support. Perhaps they told you that running away from problems is never an answer.'

It isn't exactly a ticking off. But he lets his eyes close in sorrow, as if it is.

'Perhaps the village leaf doctor, the wise man, was able to advise,' I say.

His eyes open. 'Leaf doctor, no. Leaf doctor in we village talk rabis. But fadda talk true.' I wonder which father he means. He runs his hand over his head. 'I very sorry for make madame heavy.' I let my eyes close in acknowledgement, as he did. 'But, problem finish. Him fadda show Michael straight road.'

He talks a while longer. I recognise a few words from the Bible, especially the Lord thy God, which he rolls into one word.

'I see,' I say. I don't really. But the important thing is that he's bothering to offer an explanation. The important thing is that he's back.

The family takes Michael's return better than I would have anticipated. Jim makes a comment about black people swanning off whenever it suits them, unlike white people who stay and graft till they've got the job done, but Michael takes the insult on the chin, if he even understands it.

Sarah's current bugbear is a new white boy at the school, who she says is a bully. When Michael comes into the room, her gaze slides off him the way it does with any irrelevant adult.

Chidike, due his monthly break, goes off on his ancient moped.

The same morning, Michael appears in the sitting room, where I'm drinking coffee and leafing through my Mrs Beeton for inspiration.

'Madame teach very many thing,' he says. 'All time Madame work hard, show man make sauce, make pie, make stew.'

'I enjoy our lessons, Michael.'

I glance down at a recipe for devilled eggs, wondering if that might make the blessed things more interesting.

'Yes, Madame. But this night I go make chop for Madame. Madame sit kiss him wind.'

'We'll do it together. There's no need for you to shoulder the whole burden.'

'Ah, Madame, is no burden. Is pleasure. Am make pie.'

I think of the roast chicken fiasco.

'Madame to please not worry,' he says. 'If pie rough then Michael put him leg for road.'

I laugh. Even if the pie is inedible, I won't let him go again.

When five o'clock comes, it's a novelty to be sitting with a book, a romance I picked up at the Club. But my eyes go over and over the same paragraph.

'Make sure you add enough water to the pastry,' I call through the kitchen door. 'Should I take a look?'

'Madame not work,' shouts Michael. 'Madame sit, please.'

He hands out Jim's ice cubes in a teacup, all covered in flour.

Jim and I sit on the settee, he with his whisky, me with a G & T. Eventually Jim puts his arm round me. 'Come down off the edge of your seat. You're making me nervous.'

Sarah comes in.

'Isn't it Adaku's training time?' I ask.

She shrugs. I pat the cushion and she comes over and cuddles up to me on the sofa. It hardly ever happens: the three of us sitting together, doing nothing.

The pie, when it sails into the dining room an hour later on the correct plate, with the pie slice in attendance beside it, is big and golden.

Jim gawps. He has every reason to. If it looks that good on

the outside, there's every chance it's good on the inside.

When we made the corned beef pie, I decorated it with leaf shapes. Michael obviously remembered.

'Look, Sarah,' I say, feeling proud of him. 'Little pastry birds, flying all round the edge.'

'I'll be mother, shall I?' asks Jim.

He pierces the crust. A puff of steam goes up, and a rich scent fills the air, a scent from a former life. As he transfers the first slice onto a plate, gravy pools out over white china and we all stare at filling that announces itself, not as corned beef or luncheon meat or sausage meat, but as real meat, sliding out in chunks, pink-brown and shining, from under a pastry roof.

The taste is overwhelming. Eating it is like coming home. I don't know if we all feel that, but we dine in complete silence and when we've finished there's a sense of disbelief.

'That was the yummiest thing ever,' says Sarah.

'You can say that again,' says Jim.

'You've done us proud, Michael,' I say. 'Your pastry was delicious. And that meat! Heaven on a plate. I don't know where your cousin got it, but please thank him.'

'Ah, thank is for bird, Madame,' says Michael. 'For him life finish.'

'Bird?' says Jim. 'Interesting. I wondered what sort of meat it was. Not chicken, for sure.'

A thought comes to me.

'Feather in your cap, Michael,' Jim goes on. 'Can't help thinking the Party Manager will be jealous as hell. What's wrong, love? You look as if you've seen a ghost.'

'It's nothing,' I say. And perhaps it is nothing. 'Who's for pudding? I think we've got some Walls.'

As Michael takes the remains of the pie back out to the kitchen, I rise to follow. I glance back at my satisfied family. I don't know what's to come. But tonight, if any ancestors are travelling back to the waters beneath the earth, I wish them safe passage.

Munachi Bones

My nephew, Uzondu Land Cruiser, visits me in the market. The crease of his trousers is sharp; his gold watch glints.

'Grass is growing on the roof, Uncle Bones. Do you think it is decorative, is that why you have not cleaned it?'

I look up to the corrugated iron. There is a green thatch, growing on nothing. It is a sort of miracle.

'This mud!' says my nephew. 'Children, animals, motorbikes altogether! It is unsanitary.'

'The Government is building us a new thoroughfare,' I say.

'Are you waiting for the Government to clean your roof also?'

I point at my peppers and tomatoes, polished so that they gleam red and green in the morning sun. But Uzondu is not impressed. 'Only a fool makes extra work for himself, Uncle Bones.'

Ten years ago he was a boy who had not learnt to despise things. He visited the market often. It offered a hundred more excitements than the village. He splashed in the standing water, pleaded with my sister, Abeo Bus Stop, to buy him trinkets. Nwake Neighbour gave him little animals shaped from horn. He loved them; did not say the unit price was too low to return the right level of revenue.

Then the women came, dressed like crows, and taught him how to read. They called him Oozo. 'It is hard for the white people to remember our names,' said my sister.

'The white people,' Oozo says now, 'are not really interested in onions and cassava. They want ebony heads, copper bowls.

They want hand-woven blankets.'

'How do you know what they want?' I ask.

He ignores me. 'They want to walk where it is clean. Where there are no flies.'

He picks up my broom stick and pokes the ceiling with it. Weeds rain down.

'They want their goods in plastic bags.'

I have seen this. 'Coca-cola,' I nod. 'Goat milk.'

'Not drinks! They do not want drinks in bags. They want them in bottles. Sealed, so the infection cannot enter.'

Bang, bang goes the pole. A clod of grass breaks apart on the ground.

'What infection?' I ask.

'Uncle Bones, how can I explain the world to a man who has not travelled?'

He is wrong. I have ridden many times to the next town to see my cousins. Even once to the city. But I say nothing. It is good that my nephew stays to work in the village.

Other young people leave. The city holds them, with its Marlboros; with its shoes that make women tall as men. With its WCs.

'Our town is not a bad place,' I say. 'The white man comes many miles to see it.'

He sighs. 'Do you think they are here for pleasure? They are here for the oil. They are here to build the pipeline. Oil will make our country rich. Electricity will come to our village. We will have a refrigerator, a television. Like the Americans.'

Uzondu has his likeness captured. In my sister's hut it stands. He wears a safari suit, holds his hand so the camera can see his beloved watch. His sunglasses stand on top of his head.

He has more eyes than God.

'Your grandfather walked always in a shroud,' I tell him, now. 'If he was killed on the road, it was easy for his family to bury him.'

Uzondu is not the only one, these days, to call me Uncle Bones. Before that, I was Munachi, plain and simple. Then one day as I pushed my wheelbarrow through the market, steering carefully to avoid the holes, the boy from the car parts stall yelled, 'Steady, Munachi Bones. Don't let your carrots fall in the mud!'

I hid my uncertainty about the way he addressed me. It was my name, with something added. But it seemed lesser. After that, I heard it many times. It did not matter where I went. And when they spoke my new name, I could hear the things they did not say.

When the meat-man asked, 'What size piece would you like, Munachi Bones?' I heard, 'Can you chew it without your old teeth falling out?'

When a boy stood for me on the bus, saying, 'Have my seat, Munachi Bones,' I heard, 'Sit down. Your legs are spindly. If the bus lurches, you will tumble.'

At the river, the young women began to let me go first. They drew aside, in their bright, fluttering groups. I was grateful for one thing: they did not try to help me.

Bones. It was not good, the day they pushed me a step closer to the other world. It is true I have no wife, no children. Then they would call me Father Munachi. But I have my field and my goats. And my sister has children enough for both of us.

The next day, Uzondu comes to me early when I am watering my cabbages. He wears a bright shirt. His shoes shine, but not from his own effort.

'You don't have to do this any more,' he says. 'Have a lie-in.'

'A lie-in. Is that what they have in America?'

He offers to help with the watering. 'Not on the leaves,' I tell him. 'Soak them at the root.' But he cannot bend down. His trousers are too tight. He glances towards the new pipelines, that run across the bottom of the field. Abeo Bus Stop has laid her washing on them to dry. 'This task is too time-consuming, the way you are doing it. We must find a quicker way. Or not do it at all.'

I go on watering. The dark water swells around the foot of each cabbage. I like to see them drink.

He does not go away. 'The white people are interested in our village, Uncle Bones. They want to see how we live.' The sun is rising. Its warmth touches my cheek. I thank it silently. 'They want to look at things in general.' What he says makes no sense. 'You will not have to do anything. Just sit in the corner.' The birds squabble in the cottonwood tree. 'It will take only a few minutes.' Impatience starts to unman him, as always. 'A few minutes for them to walk through your hut, Uncle Bones! Is that too much to ask?'

Time is not what is at stake. But I cannot tell him that. He is in too much of a hurry.

They arrive in my hut that very day, during the afternoon heat. So many they are, they must queue to get in. Woman and children, also. I have seen the white people at the market, but never so many, not all together. I hide my fear. I try to show a welcome. Their eyes are big, coloured. Some hold cloths to their noses.

'Is this tradition?' I whisper.

'Don't open your mouth,' says Uzondu. 'Your teeth will frighten them.'

He smiles, speaks in English, sweeps his arm round, points at the roof. Prods the straw, thumps the wall. Their eyes are big. They are like plants grown in darkness. They look thirsty.

'Should I make a tea?' I whisper.

'I told you. Sit still and keep your mouth shut.'

Is this any way for a boy to address his uncle?

But I recognise something from the market. One woman is wearing cloth the green of Ukazi leaves. It is from the stall of Chukwuma Three Shilling. He is a bad man but his cloth is beautiful. She has sewed the cloth into a dress, and a girl with shining straight hair hides behind its green waterfall.

It is the girl I smile at.

The girl stares. I remember that my teeth may be frightening. I cover them with my lips.

The mother says a word Uzondu has taught me, 'money'. She tries to push the child forward.

'What does she say?' I ask.

'She says, the old man doesn't bite.'

But the girl's eyes are sorrowful and her legs do not move. It is other children who come forward.

Their hands are full of paper money and coins. They drop them in my lap. I cannot understand it. But I am not drunk. Neither am I sleeping. It is a rain of pennies and shillings.

I cannot rest, that night. Like Chukwuma Three Shilling I sit, counting my money on the good earth floor.

In the morning, my nephew has the answer, as he has for all things. 'It is chicken feed to the white man. In his country, it buys nothing.'

As he scoops the money, he talks of the stock he will buy for our stall. He talks of leather pouffes, stuffed crocodiles, lamps made from elephant tusks.

'They will come again,' he says, ' the visitors. Different ones, next month, the month after. It takes many workers to build the pipelines. The pipelines are going right across our area.'

'What about my cabbages?' I ask. 'They wait to be eaten.'

'Feed them to your goats, Uncle Bones.'

'Greedy as my goats are, they cannot eat all my cabbages.'

Uzondu frowns. 'You are getting the wrong end of the stick. What does it matter if a few vegetables are wasted? What is important is our family's status. Look at it this way. You are not getting any younger. But now if you get sick, we do not have to rely on Abiola Leaf Doctor. We can send you to the new hospital in the city.'

I think of Onyedi Motorbike, who died because he could not breathe, and know there is much to thank Uzondu for. 'But why do they give us their money? What are they paying us for?'

'Don't worry about that.'

He takes his gold watch off and hands it to me.

'I cannot take this, I say. 'It is your number one possession.'

'It is yours now,' he says. 'Take it easy. Sit and watch time passing on its face.'

Later, I am at the market with my sister when Weke Car Parts shouts, 'Hey, Munachi Rolex! Is it true you will soon be able to watch *Dixon of Dock Green* in your village?'

'My son is a genius,' says Abeo Bus Stop.

I smile. And that is when I see them again, talking to Chukwuma Three Shilling. This time, the mother has a dress of pink and gold, the colours of the frangipani flowers. The child who would not give me money is with her. She stands frowning at the boys who run about beating the ground with sticks.

Chukwuma Three Shilling picks up a bolt of silver cloth; the mother inspects it.

I walk towards them. I snatch a small animal from the display of Nwake Neighbour.

The silver races over Chukwuma Three Shilling's fingers like a river.

I hold the small animal on my palm. The girl looks up.

'Hello, child. Would you like this bush rat? He has a stripe of fur on his back.'

I speak in my own language. I do not think she is afraid of my teeth.

The mother turns to see what is going on.

'Good morning, madame. I am Munachi Rolex, once Munachi Bones. You came with my nephew. You were my guests.'

I do not think she understands.

The girl reaches for the animal. I am happy. These animals are still a hit. I hope Nwake Neighbour fashions them for ever, whatever Uzondu may say.

But the mother pulls the girl's hand away, knocks the toy to the ground. She speaks through an angry mouth. I hear the word 'money'.

'It is a gift,' I say.

I turn to Chukwuma Three Shilling. 'Tell them it is a gift!'

He laughs his ugly laugh. His hat is stained with sweat.

'There is no fool like an old fool,' he says.

The mother swats at me as if I were a mosquito.

'I do not want money,' I say to her back. Chukwuma Three Shilling shakes his head and adds up her bill with his grubby pencil.

There is nothing I can do. I walk slowly back to our family's stall. When I turn, the girl is watching me. Then she turns to look at the silver cloth. When her eyes leave me, it is a bad feeling.

Iroko-man

The crate swung on the truck's little crane. Jim leapt to steady it, but the driver waved him back.

'Health and safety, mate,' he said, grabbing a corner with a padded hand and lowering the load onto the dolly.

'Alright in your garage,? he asked, pushing the load onto Jim's drive. Jim nodded. They had no car. 'Where's this one from?' asked the driver. 'Bit of heft to it.'

'Yep,' said Jim, remembering how it had taken six men to lift it off the truck at Calabar dock. 'It's from Nigeria. We lived there.'

'Well, they know how to make a bleedin' packing crate, I'll say that for them,' said the driver.

'It's good wood alright,' said Jim. 'Iroko. African teak, they call it.'

They called it oji wood too. Jim would have told the driver that, adding that one tribe thought the tree's spirit got trapped in the wood when you cut it down unless you said certain prayers.

But the driver was checking his watch, saying he was due in Croydon in half an hour, would you Adam and Eve it. A spasm of paperwork and he was gone.

Five other houses stood around the head of the cul de sac. Most windows had net curtains but none had so much as trembled. Jim was disappointed on the crate's behalf.

The estate was dead, with all the men at work, the children at school and the women doing, well, whatever it was women did in the late mornings. He fingered the coiled tie in his jacket pocket. He must get back to work. In the garage he pulled the rollover door down; ran his hand up the crate's side. The wood was yellowish, ordinary looking. But he'd seen oiled iroko turn rich in a matter of months. The final colour was stunning, somewhere between rose and chocolate.

It was a fresh spring day and work was a twenty minute walk. That was why they'd moved to this box on an estate so new and pink of pavement it felt no-one should really be living there.

He set off. First the uphill slog along the main road, then the turn into the long drive that led through ancient woodland, part of the grounds of the converted mansion his company occupied. Many of the trees were as old as Jim; older. Walking under their canopies, some still, some fluttering, he realised he was coming to know the different patterns of their bark and leaves. Oak, sycamore, birch, chestnut and horse chestnut: he'd borrowed his daughter's Ladybird Book to identify them.

A tough afternoon at work. The minute he got home, he invited Maureen and Sarah into the garage.

Sarah had been practising high jump in the back garden, and tearing up the new lawn. Maureen had been peeling potatoes and still held the paring knife.

'It's arrived,' said Jim as they came in together. 'Ta-da!'

'Oh my goodness,' said Maureen. 'It's enormous.'

'Isn't it,' said Jim.

'What is it?' asked Sarah. Her knees were green. She had started a new primary school, gone sports mad.

'It's our crate,' said Jim, 'remember? With all our Nigerian stuff in.'

'What stuff?' she asked.

Jim fought down irritation. 'Well, the fabrics you and Mum bought at Aba market; the carved heads and masks the man came to the house to sell.'

He remembered the man, smiling and thin, wearing a gown like the one he'd worn himself when they gave him his physics degree, except it was orange and white and embroidered round the edges. The man had set out his wares on their veranda: the ebony women's heads with features more Caucasian than African; the splintery masks, the pretty copper bowls. He'd stayed till Jim bought something. The first time, that had been three nights, the second time, three minutes.

Jim tried to think what else was in the crate.

'The big brass Calabar trays,' he said. 'The four little tables with the grooved tops, the ones you rolled ball bearings around, remember?'

He'd brought the little metal balls home from work; they'd been a big hit. Sarah had sat on the floor for hours, pushing them in columns up and down the carved table tops, her tongue sticking out in concentration.

But now she looked blank.

He tried again. 'The horn animals from the market. The bush baby, the porcupine, the giraffe?'

'Oh those,' said Sarah. She turned to her mother. 'Can I go back out now?'

'Of course you can,' said Maureen.

When she'd gone, Jim looked at his wife, wanting to say that if he'd behaved like that as a boy, he'd have been given a good hiding.

But Maureen spoke first. 'Aren't you going to open it?'

'I can't do it just like that,' said Jim. 'The lid's held down by six inch nails. I'll need a crowbar. I'll have to borrow one from work.'

'It's so big,' said Maureen. 'Where are we going to put everything?'

'You wanted a big crate,' said Jim, 'so you could get all your curtains and whatnot in.'

'Yes,' said Maureen. 'It seems a lifetime ago now.'

'It was only three months,' said Jim.

Later, he heard her talking on the phone. 'We had so much space out there,' she was saying. 'Too much, really. What made us buy all those coffee tables? Conservatory furniture's what we need now. We've got a conservatory at the new house, did I tell you?'

In February, when they'd got back, they'd gone straight down to see Jim's father in Cheltenham. Aunt Gladys had been there too.

The oldies had glazed over when Jim started talking about the family's African adventure. Dad was more interested in his own bowels and an hour into the reunion wanted to switch the TV on for a new soap opera about a motel. *Crossroads*, it was called. A stupid name. Maureen and Sarah went along with it but Jim took himself off in the cold afternoon for a walk, ending up in the shed at the bottom of the garden. He sat on a broken stool by the dirty window, remembering the fields behind the house when he was a boy, remembering his dead brother. The woodworking tools sat with him, sharp and qualified in the darkness, these days unused.

At the weekend, Jim went up the stepladder to get a purchase on the crowbar. As the nails came out, the crate groaned like a wildebeest.

When it was finally dismantled, Jim called the family in again, hoping for more interest. The big Awka pots were dramatic, he thought; the bolts of cloth bold; the carved heads alien and exciting in the concrete garage. A stuffed crocodile stared from the eerie glass beads of its eyes.

But Sarah, standing just inside the door chewing the end of a plait, looked scared. Maureen gave a nervous laugh and said it was all a bit larger than life, wasn't it, and that she'd forgotten how bush some of the craftsmanship was. She fingered the fabric and said, 'Gosh, the cotton's gaudy. And all that ironing! It's hardly drip dry.' Then she said that the pots would look alright with some nice plants in. And the heads would make a good talking point. 'When we give dinner parties,' she added.

Sarah slipped out.

'Fine,' said Jim, thinking of everyone gathered around their table, talking for hours about how some theatre critic had used the F-word on TV, or how hemlines were rising.

From the shipment, they would keep two trays, three heads, one table and two pots. He and Maureen ground out an agreement over breakfast the next morning. Then she told him that Goldie the eagle, who had escaped from London Zoo thirteen days ago, had been recaptured. Poor bugger, said Jim. And Maureen said yes, but the eagle had been in captivity for so long that it was no longer suited to a life in the wild.

The morning at work was the usual welter of internal memos to and from management. Many words; scant action, every move hedged around with ifs and buts.

Out there, six crews had lived on houseboats in the Niger Delta; had gone from there into the bush to take their readings. The locals lived with them, to tote seismometers and darkroom equipment through the mangrove swamps, to cut paths through the brush with machetes, to keep a weather eye out for elephants.

Jim had been the fixer, sent when there was a problem. He

travelled out by jeep, by motor boat, by foot. The crews were hard to find: the drivers made mistakes and sometimes he had to spend the night in a village, with pigs running in and out of his hut and a chief with scarified cheeks inviting him in to chew kola nut, an acquired taste he never quite acquired.

But once he'd found a crew, everything was simple. A problem didn't exist that he couldn't fix and people trusted his judgement. When he was helicoptered onto a rig, he could order a shut down and the client would jump to it, even though an idle rig cost thousands.

Now at his desk, back in the world of deadlines, politics and pricing, it seemed no-one trusted him. And he fixed nothing.

The bright spot was lunch. A colleague kept a bottle in his desk drawer; they had a couple of stiffeners before they hit the canteen. The colleague told jokes. They were blue but you had to laugh when you'd crewed with a bloke. Management looked over, shook their heads. Sitting there in their suits and ties and their shiny shoes, they knew fuck all, thought Jim. It made him laugh the louder.

Back home Maureen, pleased as Punch, told him she'd phoned Oxfam.

A child with flies on its face came to mind.

'They've got shops now,' said Maureen, 'and there's one opened in Bromley. They take your tat and sell it. They send the profits to Third World countries.'

She pulled him through into the sitting room where the two Awka pots now stood, one in a corner by the television and one on the hearth of the feature fireplace. They were planted up.

'Look,' she said, 'rubber plants. I got them at Wigmore's.

They're quite the thing these days, apparently.'

Jim stared at the neat columns of glossy green leaves.

'They make those rough pots look quite acceptable, don't they,' said Maureen. 'And they set the fireplace off beautifully.'

The pots were acceptable to Jim as they were and he'd always disliked indoor plants even before he'd seen these stunted versions of trees that could grow to a hundred feet in the bush, and live for a hundred years. The fake stone cladding of the fireplace was hideous and looked more so when you drew attention to it. But he couldn't say any of that, not with Maureen looking so triumphant. He gave an all-purpose grunt and retreated.

In the garage, he moved towards the great slats that now leant against the wall on the far side. Some were four foot long, some six, but they were all sturdy and broad, nothing like the planks you saw in hardware shops. The wood must have come from an old tree, he thought.

The bark of old iroko trees was scaly and grey, like dried snakeskin. The trunk was straight and the branches took a long time to start. Such a tree stood on a bend of Aba River and Jim had often stopped in his jeep to admire it. When people were hard to deal with, trees were not. In the tree's shade, the light no longer seared Jim's eyes. Leaves stirred in a breeze he hadn't noticed and the trunk shared its coolness. In the dim garage, Jim felt again the two long white catkins the tree had one day bestowed onto his head like confetti.

A sound made him jump.

Maureen stood in the doorway, outlined in the light from the kitchen.

'So this is where you've got to,' she said, in a bruised tone.

'I wanted to show you some wallpaper samples. Magnolia is all very well, but even the builders said we might want to jazz things up a little, *personalise* the house.'

'Mm,' said Jim.

'Don't you care?' she asked. She asked questions like that but never left space for an answer. 'Oxfam are coming on Monday,' she said. 'Shall I ask them to take all that wood, too?' She bustled to the chest freezer, which opened with a sucking noise. 'It's cumbersome,' she said. 'But someone might find a use for it.'

She wore her mum's faded green pinny over a black and white knee-length dress. She looked nice, Jim thought, her dark hair damp from the steamy kitchen.

'I was thinking of keeping the wood,' he said.

She stood, a bag of petit pois in her hand. 'What on earth for?'

'I could make a table,' said Jim.

Maureen stared. 'A table?'

'Or a stool,' he said. 'Or a bench. Didn't you say you needed one for the conservatory?'

'*We* need one,' said Maureen. 'Anyway, I want a nice one.'

Jim laughed. 'It will be nice.'

'But you haven't got any tools,' said Maureen.

'I'll use Dad's,' said Jim. 'He'll be glad to see them put to use.'

'You're not a carpenter,' said Maureen.

'I watched Dad as a boy,' said Jim. 'Anyway, he'll show me.' He imagined it: wielding chisel and plane under the gimlet eye.

Maureen gripped the frosted green bag, lips parted as if to voice further objections.

Jim crossed the garage and put his arm around her. 'I can make the bench to your spec. You can have it any length you like. And any width. With a back or without a back.'

'Are you sure?' she asked.

'It's not rocket science,' said Jim.

Her shoulders softened. She made herself small under his arm.

'Could it have armrests?' she asked.

'Of course it could,' said Jim.

'I'd better get the peas on,' she said.

She went out and he gazed after her, wondering at the words that had just spoken themselves. He'd never wanted to be a carpenter. Perhaps he would fail the wood. Perhaps the Iroko-man would be angered. As he closed the door, he glanced once more at the boards standing against the far wall, tall and short as a group of villagers, and nodded at them.

Heels

As she walked beside Sister Jacinta along the Ikot Ekpene Road, Sister Benedict fell into the temptation of talking.

'There must be some who find themselves unequal to the life here,' she said, gazing ahead to where the morning haze swallowed the road.

Sr Jacinta, who was principal of the school, often took her time to respond and during that time, one's words seemed more and more superfluous. They passed a roadside shrine. The Action Man inside the glass box had toppled and lay stiff against the back wall, his gun pointing at the sky. He was a long way out of sight before Sr Jacinta said, 'I take it you mean yourself, Sister Benedict.'

She began to talk about Satan and the many ways he beguiled them. As they passed the place where last week a dark mound had shimmered and now bones lay in an exploded diagram, she said, 'Making us see ourselves as inferior, well, I'm inclined to believe that's just one more of his tricks.'

The first rain of the day had darkened the road and Sr Benedict felt grit between her toes. Early though it was, inside her long white sleeve a trickle of sweat reached her elbow. The morning walk always started moisture leaking from places that she didn't even know could sweat. But since God frowned on deodorant, there was little she could do.

A month ago, she'd still been in the convent at Roscommon with its pretty gardens and green fields all around. Cows with broad rubberised noses had collected every evening at the back fence; tall stems of lavender had bowed low then bounced back when a bee took off. The spiders were so tiny that you couldn't feel them cross the back of your hand. The building itself, Victorian with high cornices and cool rooms, had kept her body dry and boosted her prayers. They had fairly sailed through the airy upper floors. The nuns had taken her in as a baby: she'd known no other home.

Here did not feel like home. She tried to pray about it, but the humidity poached her face and the low ceilings stopped her prayers, matted and tangled them.

'I fail in so many ways, Sister,' she said. 'Sometimes I even compare my own trivial sufferings to the great sufferings of Christ.'

'It's the effort that matters,' said Sr Jacinta, 'not the result. We try, with pure intentions. The rest is up to God.'

She was a shrimp of a woman. She tried to lift everyone, but didn't always succeed.

All the staff at Sancta Maria Elementary School were women. At morning assembly, with their cotton wraps and home-sewn dresses, they brought flowers, butterflies and geometric circles to the stage, making the nuns look ghostly in their white habits. The children, who wore navy and white, filed in to a piano accompaniment and stood waiting for the signal to sit.

Sr Benedict turned the pages of Sr Ermintrude's music, keeping her elbow tight in to prevent underarm odour escaping. In her desk she kept a wet flannel in a plastic bag, but its effect only lasted minutes.

The pupils descended in a rumble and Sr Benedict took her place on stage. She noticed that Mrs Hammond's chair was empty and while the school inclined its head for the Lord's Prayer, she struggled with unwelcome feelings. Mrs Hammond took Class 3D and when she was absent, Sr Benedict, whose real job was school secretary, had to fill in.

'Women's troubles,' Sr Jacinta confided after assembly. But the thought of Class 3D gave Sr Benedict troubles of her own. She wasn't the only untrained teacher in the school. Mrs Hammond and Miss Gomez were qualified only by having once been taught themselves. But she was surely the only useless one.

An hour later, standing in front of the fifteen children, her eyes went automatically to the difficult ones, both boys. Joseph, black, was slow and reluctant. Messes haunted him: stained shorts, squashed food, torn books. Johnny, white, blond and fleshy, was an out-and-out troublemaker.

'Good morning, children,' she said.

The gloss-painted desks shone in bright colours.

'Good morning, miss,' the children chanted.

They were meant to call her sister. She decided to overlook it. 'Shall we start with reading aloud? Would you like to get out your copies of *Poetry for African Schools*?'

'No,' said a voice and someone banged their desk shut.

'Gently, gently,' she warbled.

Last week a passerby had found the poetry books in a puddle outside the school gates but no-one would own up to it.

'Let's turn to page thirty-four,' she said.

It was a random choice.

'Oh dear,' she said when she saw the poem, 'The Miller'. 'I know this isn't one of your favourites. But it's on the syllabus, I'm afraid, so we have to tackle it. We will go round the class, taking two lines each. Joseph, please begin.'

Joseph groaned. 'Miss, I cannot.'

Why did it have to be this class, where no-one wanted to learn? Other teachers boasted about excellent spelling scores; pupils doing extra reading in their own time. 'Of course you can, dear. Just read the first line.' Joseph gawped at the page. 'Try and pronounce the words as you see them written. It doesn't matter if you don't get them exactly right.'

'We'll all help you,' she added, without confidence.

Vertical lines appeared on Joseph's brow.

Sr Benedict wondered suddenly if he could read. Basic literacy was an entrance requirement, but if a father was a local chief, Sr Jacinta sometimes waived it. Fresh sweat broke out on her back and scalp.

'The miller's mill-dog,' she said quickly. 'Now, what was the miller's mill-dog doing, Joseph? Perhaps we can guess. What do dogs often do?'

Joseph remained silent.

A hand went up. 'Miss, miss!' It was Johnny.

Sr Benedict let her gaze hover, waiting for someone different to volunteer. No-one did.

'Alright, Johnny,' she said.

Johnny gave a sly smile. 'They go pee-pee, miss.'

Several children sniggered, though some looked shocked. Sr Benedict pressed her lips together. Strictly speaking, the answer was correct. She gave a crisp nod. 'Yes, they go pee-pee.'

Laughter erupted all round the classroom. She had made a mistake in repeating it, she thought. She wished she was in her office, opening post and composing routine letters to parents.

'But what else do they do?' she said. 'What do they do in the heat?'

The laughter stopped but hands failed to rise. 'The answer

is in the book in front of you,' said Sr Benedict. 'Use your eyes!'

'Dey scratch off dem tsetse fly,' someone called.

'Dem gets sick an die!'

At least they were making suggestions, thought Sr Benedict. But they weren't supposed to shout things out. Nor were they supposed to use Pidgin in class. Fifteen minutes in, misdemeanours were mounting and she didn't know which to tackle first. The noise level rose. Last time, Mrs Engurube had had to come in from next door. She'd silenced them in a voice that had made Sr Benedict herself freeze and sit up straight. Mrs Engurube's frilly blouse, tight skirt and pink high-heeled slingbacks hadn't detracted from her authority, but only added to it.

'Dem sweat like a Christmas goat,' yelled Johnny.

'Silence in class,' Sr Benedict shrilled. 'What is the dog doing *in the poem*?'

Johnny pinched his nose between his thumb and forefinger and said, 'Da biller's bill-dog lay at de bill door and his dabe was little Bingo.'

Sr Benedict went hot then cold. She stared at the boy, not knowing whether he was aping the Pidgin speakers or making a point about her own body odour. Either way she should crack down on him, hard.

But she had no idea how to.

'Take your hand away from your face,' was all she managed to say. 'Turn to the poem on the facing page please, class. "London Bridge is Falling Down".'

The rest of the lesson was a write-off. The children read 'London Bridge' and all the poems following in exaggerated accents, breaking frequently into giggles.

When the bell went, Sr Benedict broke for the staff toilets where she ran the tap onto a wad of toilet paper, went into a cubicle and stripped to the waist. She washed and dried herself then rubbed a bar of soap hard under her arms, no matter what God thought.

Later that day, Sr Benedict discovered that she was not the only teacher to find Johnny difficult. Called to the principal's office to take notes, she sharpened her pencil while Mrs Engurube, hair high under a leopard print scarf, stood in front of Sr Jacinta's desk waving her hands about. Above them the ceiling fan worked the air as if it was a stiff batter.

Johnny had stolen some plasticine.

The discussion went back and forth. When St Jacinta said the plasticine had been old, Mrs Engurube said fresh sticks had been taken from Mrs Gomez' cupboard. When Sr Jacinta said the boy was only eight and that his mother had been sent back to England with malaria, Mrs Engurube said theft was theft. The rhinestones in her long earrings caught the light and made Sr Benedict think of all the jewellery she'd never worn herself because they were pure adornment, the marks of this world.

The argument grew heated, on Mrs Engurube's side anyway.

'Johnny should be suspended,' she suddenly said. Sr Benedict let out a gasp.

Both women looked at her.

'Only, it is so difficult for a child to be without a mother,' said Sr Benedict.

Mrs Engurube stared as if she was a dog who had somehow managed to speak.

Sr Benedict returned to her note-taking.

The discussion continued until Sr Jacinta played her ace. Compassion, she said, was the primary Christian virtue and as such, it should underpin every decision that was taken in the school.

Mrs Engurube knew when she was beaten. She pressed her lips together as if resenting how Christ had to be brought in to it all the time but all she said was, 'A child you carry on your back will not know how far the journey is.'

The next day, when Mrs Hammond was absent again, Sr Benedict learnt that she must mark and return the class' Intensive Writing homework. Then she was to introduce joined up writing.

She sat in her office. Outside, three vultures, bald and cloaked, perched on the toilet block. The exercise books lay before her, open in a wide pile. 'Against your father's warning you are sailing downriver in a small boat,' she read. 'You rush towards the edge of a waterfall. What do you see, feel and hear?'

Violent, she thought. But the topics were ratified by the Eastern Nigeria Ministry of Education, and must not be tampered with.

She read several essays. Only a few pupils had used description, and none showed any fear at meeting death by drowning. Perhaps they were too young. All she was able to do was to mark their spelling and comment on the neatness or otherwise of their writing.

But the next essay was very different. After the boat had gone over the edge of the waterfall, a sea spirit took the writer to live in a palace on the ocean bed where they played in ship wrecks and lived happily ever after. Sr Benedict felt a spasm of interest. Local gods were out of bounds so she would have to penalise that. But she could award marks for imagination. The author was probably one of the quieter girls. She turned the book over. Johnny Piper, it said, underlined twice.

The class didn't object to her marks, probably because they were far more generous than Mrs Hammond's would have been. 'C' was her lowest. It was still the highest mark Joseph had ever received. Johnny got a 'B+'. She hoped he'd be pleased. But when she handed his book over and congratulated him, his face was so dead she thought he hadn't heard. She reached out, not really to touch him, but he jerked away from her, alive after all.

The joined-up writing exercise started reasonably well. She explained the task, then copied shapes from the text book onto the board. The class settled quickly, some even smiling as they worked. She was surprised. She felt her shoulders go down a millimetre or two. She thought she might talk to Johnny after the lesson; ask him about his story.

But then the atmosphere changed. When the second hand of the clock ticked round to 1.45 exactly, every pupil in the room opened their desks, creating a wall of shiny multicoloured lids. Sr Benedict's mouth fell open.

'But, but,' she said, knowing that even though it wasn't a crime to open your desk, if you did it at the same time as fourteen other people, it somehow became so. Or did it? For one giddy moment, she thought she might ignore it. But she could not imagine Mrs Engurube ignoring it. Class 3D, however, would never try such a thing with Mrs Engurube.

By the time she had thought all this, laughter, which to that point came in isolated and muffled explosions, had turned open and shrill. She told them to stop it, but they seemed helpless, almost hysterical. She found herself pleading with them to tell her what she'd done to deserve such treatment. A boy flailed on the floor pretending to have a fit, and she could only stare at him in horror. She could no more stop what was happening than she could lift up her arms and ascend to Heaven.

'Turn over a new leaf with the class', was Sr Jacinta's advice at the weekend. 'Ask God to help you forget all that is past and gone.'

Eating with the other nuns, who seemed to recognise her as a human being, Sr Benedict began to believe this was possible. She remembered the miracle of her flight here: how quickly Ireland had shrunk in the oval window; how, when the plane had reached the sky, the sky had still been above them, plain and cloudless as blue paint. It was all still to play for, she realised. She imagined fresh starts with rewarding outcomes; almost hoped that next week Mrs Hammond would still be absent.

On Monday morning, when the last teacher had climbed the creaking steps and taken her place on stage, Sr Benedict saw, by the fact that Mrs Engurube now sat next to Mrs Gomez, that not only was Mrs Hammond absent, but her chair had been removed. The sight made Sr Benedict's eyes widen, her breath catch. God had read her thoughts. God had perhaps taken her too seriously.

As soon as she entered the classroom of 3D, the optimism she'd felt earlier blew away like dandelion fluff. She knew immediately that while she'd tried to forget last week, last week had made a point of not forgetting her. It had roosted in the class, who didn't react when she came in, but stayed yawning and draped over their desks, flicking things.

Above the blackboard stood a picture of Christ, parting His robes to bare the glowing ruby of His heart. Sr Benedict glanced to Him for help. As she did, she noticed that something had been written on the blackboard. The letters were badly formed. Some were joined and some weren't. But the spelling was surprisingly accurate. 'Cleanliness is next to Godliness', it said. Beneath, the board rubber lay on its back, fuzzed with chalk dust.

Sr Benedict turned to the class. Their faces blurred and splintered in her eyes, and the room leapt behind them. Out of her mouth came words that made no sense. Then she ran.

The heat on the Ikot Ekpene Road was fierce. When Sr Benedict got to the shrine, with its doll in dusty camouflage helmet and black boots, she had to stop to lean on her thighs, gasping. It took a while to get her breath back and make herself set off again at a steadier pace.

She heard the rasp of a moped behind; stepped aside to let it pass.

But the moped stopped. She turned, shading her eyes. Astride it was Mrs Engurube, in her frilled blouse and leopard print headscarf, skirt hitched nearly to her waist.

'Where are you going, sister?' the teacher asked.

Sr Benedict sighed. 'That's no business of yours, Mrs Engurube. I suppose Sister Jacinta sent you. Well, you can tell her she's wasting her time.' She paused. 'God bless her,' she crossed herself.

The teacher's many bracelets tinkled as she got off the bike. She hitched up the strap of a pink sling-back that had slipped down. 'The Ibibe boy done pepper me,' she said. 'I come out from the classroom to take five. That's when I see you run.' She fished a lace square from somewhere and dabbed moisture off her forehead and cheeks. She jerked her head at the passenger seat. 'Where you wan go?'

'Thank you,' said Sr Benedict. 'But I am better on foot.'

'No, no, the heat is very bad,' said Mrs Engurube. 'For English people.'

'I'm not English,' said Sr Benedict. 'I'm Irish.'

'I see,' said Mrs Engurube, regarding her. 'Then we will walk together.'

'But what about your class?' asked Sr Benedict. 'What about the Ibibe boy?'

What about yours, she expected the teacher to shoot back. But Mrs Engurube just pushed the moped onto the bleached grass at the side of the road and kicked down its stand.

They set off. Within minutes it was obvious that the teacher couldn't keep up; her heels made her totter on the disintegrating road. Sr Benedict had to slow her pace, which made the sun bear down on them harder. A transparent patch grew on the front of Mrs Engurube's blouse. Her walk turned into a hobble.

It was an age before they reached the tall mesh gate of the community building. Beyond, washing dried on the line, and Sr Ermintrude's vegetable patch soaked up a recent watering.

Sr Benedict's face was slippery, burning. She forced out a thank you. 'It was decent of you, Mrs Engurube.' That much was true.

'It is not a problem to me,' said the teacher, mopping her cheeks.

Perhaps she expected to be invited in and offered a cold drink. But Sr Benedict's army surplus bed had never seemed so alluring. All she wanted was to lie down, close her eyes and doze like the dogs in the shade of the house opposite. Beyond that, nothing.

'I'll be getting in then,' she said. The gate clanged as she slid the bar open. She stepped inside but could not close it, not with Mrs Engurube still standing there.

'The heat is fierce indeed when you stand still,' said Sr Benedict.

'You are right,' said Mrs Engurube and turned. Sr Benedict raised silent thanks to God. The teacher had meant well. But if people were going to insist on wearing high heels, they should not go gallivanting up and down pot-holed roads.

Sr Benedict shook her head at the very idea of those ridiculous, impractical shoes. But as the teacher walked away, she noticed something that made her gasp: their straps were no longer pink.

'Mrs Engurube! Mrs Engurube, stop!' she called. 'Your heels. They are bleeding! Your shoes are covered in blood.'

But the teacher raised her arm and carried on walking. Had she heard?

'Stop,' called Sr Benedict again. 'You will cripple yourself. Cecilia, stop!'

The teacher did not stop.

Sr Benedict glanced with longing at the community building. Inside was the simple chapel, the quiet sitting room with its elaborately carved iroko tables and Christ looking down from a cross made of the same dark wood. Inside was the bedroom where unobserved, she could rest her face.

Out here was the unforgiving sun, the crumbling road and a headstrong woman moving slowly out of earshot. If Sr Benedict was going to go after her, she should go now.

Gold Cloth

On her first visit to the bone-dry marketplace, she squinted at the fabric the way her mother always did. She ran her thumb-nail across it; saw how it seemed to shift in the sun. What she was looking for, she didn't know – her mother was secretive – but she'd seen these actions impress Gloucester stall holders.

The man stepped from behind his multicoloured bolts of cloth and snatched the fabric out of her hands. 'Madame not damage, if madame not want buy.'

'But I'm trying to see what sort of material it is!'

'Madame want information, madame ask please.'

He was short and thick bodied and the edge of his yellow embroidered hat was dark with sweat. They called him Chuk-wuma Three Shilling.

The sun was like an iron bar on her shoulders. Women pushed past, their string bags full of knobbly brown roots. They all wore headscarves. Perhaps she should get one. 'So, what sort of material is it?'

'What type of material madame wish?'

'Just tell me what it is.'

'Is high quality ny-lone, madame. Plenty fine cloth. Real bottom box.'

She put it down. 'I want silk. Or rayon.' She knew these were better than nylon.

'Exactly. Quality ny-lone silk rayon.'

She sighed. 'How much?'

'Three shilling per yard, madame.'

She opened her purse, then remembered you had to bargain. If you didn't, they would despise you. They hated the Americans, who paid whatever they were asked straight away.

'I'll give you one and six,' she said.

'Pah,' said the stallholder. 'Three shilling is my price. I have ten child, two wife, three mudda, one fadder to feed.'

'That's a lot of mothers,' she said.

He didn't smile.

She looked again at the fabric. She liked it, and out here she didn't like much. Local shillings were worth less than British shillings. And there must be circumstances in which you didn't barter, although when she'd said this at the British Club, the other wives had talked about distorting the local economy.

'Okay, okay,' said the stallholder. 'Two shillings and a half.'

She hid her surprise. 'Two shillings. I'll give you two shillings.'

The stallholder frowned. 'My fadda, one arm and half him leg blown off.'

'Oh dear.'

'In war, fighting for British cause.'

She opened her purse.

After lunch, when Jim and Sarah went for their siesta, she slid the heavy gold slab out of the brown paper bag. Like insects' wings, its colour held the ghosts of other colours – rose, purple, olive. They chimed with the reddish oji wood of the dining table.

She unfolded the ingot, smoothing as she went. She wondered again what it was. She wished she were more practical. The basic craft skills were what you needed here, sewing and making things. The other wives said that it was the only way to have anything nice.

She opened the sewing basket, a wicker casket with gilt fastenings that had come all the way from the cupboard under her mother's stairs. In the kitchen, the fridge laboured to keep cool.

The pinking shears had smooth black handles. She slipped her fingers into them and surveyed the gold sea of fabric before her. The uninterrupted colour brought a settled feeling to her shoulders.

The sofa and chairs had ten cushions and they were all square so it was only a question of cutting backs, fronts, and strips to join them. Before starting, she snipped a long strip from the ragged end, folded it into a small package and stashed it in the basket. She might try and make an evening dress for Rita, the Sindy doll.

She made the first long cut. The shears ground on the table top and the fabric melted away each side of their broad molars.

She cut and cut until a deep pink weal glowed on one of her fingers. The pile of zigzag-edged squares mounted.

Her sewing machine, a present from Jim, was a Bernina, electric. He'd found it at the local hardware store, Rock of Ages & Sons. At first she'd hated it. It was nothing like her mother's Singer, with its black voluptuous body, gold lettering and cast-iron treadle. And he'd bought it to help her settle, a double-edged sword.

But then she'd mended a pair of his shorts, and had appreciated the neatness and speed of its stitching. Its efficiency was contagious: made her feel like a magician.

She pinned two glossy squares together.

A high-pitched sound came from outside. She stood and crossed the open plan sitting room to the window. She looked up and down the Ikot Ekpene road, expecting to see an animal wounded or dying.

Perhaps it was the juju men, who came some afternoons to the door dressed in sacking and grass skirts, or wearing black masks painted with eyes and tongues. One carried a glass shrine on his head, with a doll in it. They danced and drummed until Jim paid them to go away.

But the road ran its usual deserted course, flanked by scrubland and telegraph poles with no wires. The Chevrolet stood on the road pointing towards Port Harcourt. Jim wouldn't park it in the drive, joking that they might have to get away quickly in the middle of the night. Well, she assumed it was a joke.

She sat down and fed the material under the machine's foot. She thought about England, and how, before they left three weeks ago, they'd gazed at the country's pastel segments and torn edge of coastline in their World Atlas; had pointed at long rivers and curious names, and laughed. The oil company's Essentials list had taken her down unfamiliar streets behind Gloucester Cross, into dark slices of shops, to come out with mosquito nets, iodine, salt tablets. It had felt like a real adventure.

And it was an adventure for Sarah, who was already adjusting; had made a friend at school. Jim complained about having to carry heavy equipment through the mangrove swamps, but he ate and slept as he never had in England. Some of the wives seemed completely at home, drinking and lording it over the new arrivals. Maureen wondered what was wrong with her, that she couldn't just pull herself together and enjoy her new life here with her good husband and the one child she had been granted.

She seamed the cushion on three sides, yanked the work out of the machine and snapped the threads with her teeth.

She heard the sound again. It wasn't from an animal, she

realised, and it had come from the back. She went to the French doors and peered down the compound. Beyond the cracked red mud, that she was trying to turn into a garden, stood the concrete block where their servant Chidike lived. Behind, stretched a rough hedge of jungle geranium. Then came the golf course with its lumpy red termite hills. She opened one of the doors.

As she turned back into the room, the sound came again, long and clear. It made the hairs of her forearms stand up. It was a woman. It was coming from the servants' block.

She should go upstairs and wake Jim. Instead, she found herself in the kitchen, pushing open the screen door, hurrying out into the fierce heat.

When she got to the hut, still clutching the gold cover, she remembered that she'd never been inside, that Jim didn't like her to visit without him. Or with him. That Chidike invited friends over to play poker with racy cards. But the shrill cries, more regular now, seemed to reach inside her. She was through the bead curtain in a second.

It was hot and muggy inside the hut, and smelt of newly turned soil. She couldn't see. Then a low dark shape rose towards her.

Yesterday, one of the juju men had come to the doorstep dressed as Ogbunabali, the Igbo god of death. His black mask was painted with the god's long curved teeth, his lolling red tongue and eyes: one big, one small.

Ogbunabali came to Maureen now, and she stepped back with a little cry.

'Madame.'

She smelt Chidike's hair ointment; breathed out.

'Sorry. You startled me.'

'What is the problem, Madame?' asked Chidike. 'Something is happen in the house? You want for I to come?'

'No,' she said. 'I thought someone was unwell.'

She tried to peer around him.

Chidike shook his head. 'Is nothing for to worry Madame or Master.'

But Maureen's eyes were adjusting to the dark. A girl was humped on a mattress at the back of the room, her face to the wall.

Her skin prickled. Had she disturbed them in an intimacy? She'd heard, from her friend who was a nurse, that Africans practised 'dry sex' and that it sometimes hurt both parties, especially the woman.

The girl was struggling to turn over. As she did, she made a glottal sound. Maureen had never touched Chidike, even to shake his hand, but she shoved him out of the way and ran to the mattress. She saw that the girl's thin flowered dress was sodden at the back.

'I say, is nothing for to worry Madame or Master,' said Chidike again.

The girl's face shone with sweat. She felt clammy to the touch. She looked about twelve or thirteen.

'This my sister,' said Chidike. She come stay one day, two day.'

The girl rolled onto her back and let out another wail. Tears coursed from the sides of her eyes.

'She needs a doctor,' said Maureen.

'There is doctor in we village.'

'Not that sort of doctor. She needs to go to the hospital. Can you get her there?' Chidike looked at the floor. 'Not on the motorbike. In the car.'

She must have raised her voice. The girl seemed to notice her for the first time. Maureen took her hand, dropping the shining cloth at the girl's side. The girl's hand was hot and slippery. Maureen pressed it. 'Breathe,' she said. 'Try and breathe. Do you know what breathe means?'

The girl did not seem to hear. She was gazing at the cushion cover, which gleamed softly beside the mattress.

Maureen picked it up and held it out. It shone in her hand, not gold as it was outside, but unearthly silver.

The girl took the cloth. '*Onwa, onwa,*' she said.

Incredibly, she smiled.

'What did she say?' asked Maureen.

Chidike did not reply.

The girl still smiled. But the pains would come again. They would come and come, worse and worse, until it was all over.

She turned to Chidike. 'How far gone was she?'

'Gone?'

'With child.'

'No. No,' said Chidike. 'She is sister only.'

'It's not a judgement. The doctor will ask.'

'*Na na itibe.*'

'What?'

'Let the eagle perch. Let the hawk perch.'

She stared at him. 'Look, you won't have to pay, if that's what you're worried about. I'll pay.' He surveyed the ground. 'Are you going to help? Are you going to help or not?'

The thought came to Maureen that she could drive. She had no licence. But she had driven once, during the war, because she'd had to. The car was an automatic, and there was little traffic on the roads. She jumped to her feet.

'I'm going to get the car. Can she walk a little? Can she walk, do you think?'

She didn't wait for an answer.

As she left the hut, Chidike said something sharp to the girl, in his own language. It made Maureen run all the faster, through the baking compound to the kitchen, where she snatched the keys from the nail.

She didn't know what Chidike had said. But it would be something about not making a fuss. They hated it when you made a fuss. The husbands, the brothers, the doctors. And then even the nurses, women like yourself, as they hauled mauled sheets out from under you.

The handle of the car door was red hot. She bound her handkerchief around her hand to open it. Inside, the heat was thick and she had to force herself in. The Naugahyde seared the backs of her legs.

Jim was running towards her in his pale blue pyjama bottoms, the buckles of his sandals flapping. 'What's going on?'

'Chidike's sister is ill.'

'Uh?'

Sarah, in her white nightdress, wandered onto the front porch.

'We've got to get her to hospital.'

In her husband's presence, a lot of the things she said sounded silly. The hospital might be this side of Enugu, she heard him think, but it was ninety miles away down roads that would take forever.

Still, she turned the keys in the ignition. The car was a hot cage.

'But you can't even drive!' said Jim. 'And I need the car. I'm meeting a client at two. He's flown out specially.'

'She's having a miscarriage,' said Maureen.

Jim's mouth fell open; he stepped back. Even the word frightened him. She almost laughed. She reversed the car then kangarooed it as far as the back door, which was where the drive ran out. Leaving the engine running, she got out and ran down the compound.

As she ran, the monkey chattered on the end of its chain and threw a handful of something at her, seeds or stones, but they fell short.

At the hut, the bead curtain had been hooked to one side. She ran in, eyes swimming in darkness.

She felt before she saw that the room was empty. The table stood with its fork and cup and rolled sleeping mat beneath. The mattress had gone.

She couldn't believe it. She looked up at the ceiling as if Chidike and the girl might be up there, sitting one in one corner, one in another.

She went outside and walked around the hut. Chidike's motorbike was gone. The mattress stood against a side wall. The large dark stain was ragged, like the map of a country. She touched it, cool and sticky. She wondered if the lost baby had a soul, and if the girl had given it a name. No-one would know that name, only her.

She walked slowly to the back hedge and stared across the golf course. She tried to imagine the girl riding pillion over it, clutching Chidike all the way back to the village.

She went back into the hut and sat on the floor where the mattress had been.

She wanted to cry.

But a thought had flown into her mind and out again, like a bird flying in one window and out of another and she found herself trying to recollect it. She could not bring it back. But its spirit stayed, of something to be glad about, something good among the bad things.

Milk

When Miss Boorman brought in the blue plastic crate, the children milled around it.

'One at a time, please,' shrilled the teacher.

Sarah went to the back of the queue hoping something might happen before her turn, like Miss Boorman dropping dead. She didn't like milk. Here in England they kept it by the radiator. The thought of the thickened band of yellow and the way it clogged the straw made her go hot and cold.

When she arrived at the crate, there were two bottles left. She practically stopped breathing.

'Lucky Miss Nigeria,' said the teacher. She had been the first to call Sarah by that name and now everyone did.

'But I only want one,' said Sarah.

Since she'd started at this school last month, she'd lived in dread of Miss Boorman speaking to her. She found out now that it was worse when she didn't speak; when she pressed her orange lips together and looked at you over the top of her winged glasses.

Sarah took both bottles.

It stank in the boys' cloakroom. Geoffrey Millmar sat at the end of the row of shoe bags hung high and low. Sarah joined her second queue of the morning. Girls with empty bottles pushed past, their cheeks mottled. Geoffrey Millmar had probably made them kiss him, or made them stand still while he gave them a Chinese burn. The forfeits could be anything. Sometimes he made you curtsey. Sometimes he gave you a mission, like putting a doggy do on Miss Boorman's chair.

But the forfeits were better than the ruler, which was what the teachers gave you.

His face was spattered with freckles. Everyone thought of him as fat, even though he wasn't. When Sarah reached him, his eyes were glassy; his lips pearled with milk.

His eyes took in the two bottles. 'I can't drink *both*,' he said.

Sarah clutched the vile milk. She'd have thrown it out through the swing door except she'd already been caught doing that once. Then you had to hold your palm flat in front of the rest of the class. You felt their eyes as the ruler went up. They gasped when it snapped down, but it didn't make them like you. And your palm went purple and stung like a million wasps.

'What do you want?' she asked.

'*You* know,' said Geoffrey Millmar.

Sarah wanted to cry. At Sancta Maria, she'd looked forward to morning break, to the groundnut man and his brazier. Clutching a penny with a hole in the middle, she'd raced across the compound, beating even her friend Omo in the race for the first newspaper cone of roast nuts, hot and oily.

'I won't,' she said now. 'And you can't make me.'

Geoffrey Millmar wore a big watch with stupid dials in it. He looked at it and shrugged. Any minute now, the bell would go.

'It's dangerous,' said Sarah. 'We'd get caught. '

He shrugged.

'Pick someone else,' said Sarah.

'They're all thickoes,' said Geoffrey Millmar.

In Nigeria, you didn't call someone a thicko. You called them a Dundee United. Geoffrey Millmar was a Dundee United, which was why Miss Boorman was threatening him with the re-medial class.

Sarah glanced at the only other girl left in the cloakroom. She had plaits and a white Alice band. The girl looked away.

'I'll drink six of your milks free,' said Geoffrey Millmar.

'Ten,' said Sarah.

Geoffrey Millmar pulled the straws out and enlarged the foil openings with his thumbs. He drank both bottles in a matter of seconds. He wiped his mouth and looked pleased with himself. Booze man, thought Sarah. It was one of Omo's insults.

In the canteen, the mash had lumps. Sarah pushed it to the side of her plate. Beetroot, tapioca, meat that went round and round in your mouth: England served it all. Miss Boorman loomed, waiting while Sarah transferred atoms of potato to her mouth.

'Eat it, don't play with it,' said the teacher, swiping the fork and plunging it into the greyish clump.

Sarah took in the forkful; tried to swallow. But the big gobbet rose back up, bringing after it a hot stream that splashed onto her plate. She stood up, but a second wave came. It broke all over Miss Boorman's brown lace-ups.

The teacher stood by the desk holding up two green exercise books. One looked as if a mouse had been nibbling it.

'It has come to my attention,' she said, 'that one child from this class copied from another child – *plagiarised* their work during yesterday's spelling test.'

Plagiarised. The children looked at each other. It must be a bad thing.

'How did I discover this infringement?' asked Miss

Boorman. She jabbed a finger at a page. 'I discovered it because someone who should know better made a preposterous mistake and another child copied it verbatim.'

Infringement, preposterous, verbatim. The puzzling words piled up, speaking of the ruler, of detentions, of being made to sit on the cold lino floor outside the headmistress' office.

The teacher turned to the blackboard and picked up the board rubber. Geoffrey Millmar ducked, but not in time. Sarah heard the clop as the wood hit his head. The boy didn't move or make a sound, but tears spurted from his eyes.

Sarah's exercise book landed on the desk in front of her, making her jump.

'To the front,' said the teacher, 'with your chair.' Sarah's face burnt. She stood up, not understanding. The teacher grabbed her arm; marched her and the chair into a corner. 'Up.'

Sarah sat on the chair. The class tittered.

'Did I say sit?'

'No, miss.'

Sarah tried kneeling.

'I said *up*,' said Miss Boorman. 'Stand! Face the wall. And stay there for the rest of the lesson, or you'll be back up there tomorrow *and* the day after.'

She turned back to the class.

Sarah swayed and trembled on the shiny wood seat, not daring to touch the back. The teacher's voice rose and dropped; the blackboard chalk went dot-dot-dash. She was going to fall off. Hot-tap-cold-tap went her legs. Outside, no-one knew what was happening. A lawnmower snarled; a dog barked; a car honked. Inside, she faced the white wall.

When Miss Boorman finally said to get down, the room was

empty and the other teacher, Mr Kendal, was there, saying Judith really, is this strictly necessary. He lifted Sarah under her armpits and set her down but when her legs touched the floor, they gave way.

Mr Kendal peered at her. Why did all teachers wear glasses? 'Is this girl alright?' he asked.

'Miss Nigeria is playing the goat,' said Miss Boorman.

She turned to Sarah. 'Get up and get out.'

In the playground, the others clustered around her, firing questions like why did you come to England if you're Nigerian and how did you learn to speak English. She told them she was English and that Nigerians were black, not white. She told them she'd been born in Gloucester Infirmary.

She hoped they'd stop hating her then, but they shouted liar, liar, and grabbed sand from the sandpit to throw at her.

It was Friday. At morning break, Sarah went to the boys' cloakroom and joined the two other girls already waiting. They stood in a neat line and no-one spoke.

The first girl handed over her bottle. Geoffrey Millmar drank, and burped into her face. The girl jerked her head back and caught it on one of the coat pegs. Her face went red but she could only cry a bit or someone would want to know why. The second girl had to kneel and kiss Geoffrey Millmar's smelly Startrights. She rose with dirty smudges on the knees of her white tights. She would get into trouble for that. Sarah tried to decide which forfeit was worse.

Geoffrey Millmar's head bore the dark red mark of the board rubber. It looked sore. He would blame her for it. Her wrist felt weak as she held out her bottle.

But when he made to take it she found herself lifting it up, out of his reach.

His freckled lips, wet with milk, parted in surprise.

Sarah was surprised too. She found herself pulling the straw out of the bottle and shaking the drops of milk onto the floor; pushing her thumb into the cap and feeling the milk well up around it.

Geoffrey Millmar, thinking perhaps she was preparing it for him, held out his hand again.

Still she gripped the smooth bottle.

He looked at her from his throne of coats. 'Give,' he said.

But Sarah brought the bottle to her own lips. She took a gulp of the lukewarm milk. It was gross. But steeling herself to cope, she drank and swallowed, drank and swallowed until nothing was left in the bottle but a white veil, sliding slowly downwards.

Stones

First, Johnny didn't recognise her voice. Then he didn't sound as pleased as she'd hoped. 'Oh, right,' he said. 'We met in the veggie cafe, yeah? Look, I've got some people here. I'll call you back later.'

'Later' was a treacherous word, always hopping one step ahead, like a frog on a garden path. At midnight, after scraping orange anaglypta off her bedroom walls all evening, it became exhausted for the day.

He didn't ring that week, the next. Or if he did, he didn't leave a message.

One Friday evening, as she was getting in from work, Sainsbury's bags striping her fingers, the phone rang. 'Sarah? Sorry about the other night. Had stuff on. Busy few weeks.'

Dumped, apples rolled out and made their way across the lino.

Sarah sat down on an unpacked box. 'No problem.'

'How're you doing?'

'Fine. Good, actually.'

Pause.

'So what can I do for you?' he asked.

'Oh. Well, it was just what you said in the cafe about showing me your place. With your decor and everything. And doing it up ecologically.'

It hadn't felt lame at the time, crushed together at the tiny table in the lunchtime rush hour.

'Oh, the house,' he said. 'The organic paint. Yeah. Thing is,

I'm a bit tied up this weekend.'

'It doesn't matter,' she said. 'Sorry to bother you.'

'What're you doing now?'

'Now? I've just got in from the hospital.'

'I mean tonight.'

Her heart swam and sank at the same time. 'Tonight?'

'Yeah. Thing is, I was thinking of going skating. Over at Silver Blades. You could come along if you want.'

She hadn't skated since she was ten. She remembered how the ground slid out from under you, a tablecloth pulled by a magician.

'Where's Silver Blades?' She played for time.

'Not far. They do a special evening on a Friday night,' he said. 'For adults.' He was being spontaneous, she thought. She often wished she was more spontaneous. 'We could go for a curry afterwards,' he went on, 'if you fancy.'

'Oh,' she said. 'I haven't been for a curry up here yet. I don't know the area at all.'

'Cool.' It seemed she had agreed. 'Can you pick me up?' he asked. 'You did say you drove, didn't you?' Pause. 'Give you a chance to see my place. That was what you wanted, wasn't it?'

His street was in a warren of back to backs that faced straight on to the pavement, like people standing looking out of their own windows. She'd never seen those sorts of houses down South. The neighbourhood she'd moved into here in Manchester was tatty but it was a step up from this. His front door was purple and peeling, and she had to put her hand through the burglar bars to knock. When he opened the door, her heart flipped: tanned bare feet; tangled red-gold hair in a loose ponytail. He stood behind the bars in a warm oblong of light. Behind him were exposed floorboards and faded floral wallpaper that stopped halfway up.

'Hi,' she said.

He grinned. Keys clanked as he fiddled with the door grille, which had a lock of its own.

'You found it alright, then.'

The grille swung open, and she stepped into the small front room. A punch bag stood centre stage, at its base a plump red glove like a cartoon heart. A bare bulb hung down. He began to go through the locking process in reverse.

'We're going out, right?' she asked.

'But you want to see the place?' She nodded. 'Got to lock up then. Got mugged a few weeks back. Been careful ever since.'

'Here, on your own street?'

'My own doorstep. Had my hands full, left the door open, next thing I was face down on the floor, three kids running off up the street. Swiped my wallet and my keys.'

'How awful,' she said, to the back of his legs above her on the stairs. The stairs were bare with scuffed white paint at the edges. 'Were you hurt?'

'Little fuckers.'

'You must have felt really violated.' He didn't reply. 'Did the police get them?'

'Local kids. They live round the corner. Everyone knows 'em.'

They were on the landing now, passing a bathroom with no door. In the main bedroom, she glimpsed surfboards propped against a wall. Behind, another door stairs rose. He turned and grinned. 'No shoes allowed. Sorry.'

In the attic, he switched on the light and she saw turquoise walls. It was the only finished room in the house, he said. He described the paints he'd used; how badly they'd dripped; how long they'd taken to dry.

But she was looking at the stones. Scores of them arranged on the cobalt floorboards, some the size of a fist, others as big as cats. Their colours were dusty: sand, cream, grey. Limestone, flint, millstone grit, she didn't know. All smooth. Handfuls of pebbles glowed in a glass bowl of water by the chimneybreast. Amber, turquoise, jet.

Apart from the stones, a navy floor cushion, and four fat unlit candles on saucers, the room was empty. She pictured her own flat, at the top of a roomy Victorian semi. What with the new job, she hadn't unpacked properly and clothes still spilled out of black bin bags; teaspoons hid at the bottom of unlabelled boxes. She tried to imagine living in a space like this and couldn't.

'Wow,' she said, 'Minimal. Where did all the stones come from?'

'Beaches. It's a sort of meditation. Walking in the sun or the rain or whatever. Picking one up, putting it down. Going on to the next. Trying to find the perfect one. A bit like women.'

She waited for a laugh or a smile to soften the remark but it didn't come. Instead, he crouched, and picked up a salmon pink stone, circled by a white line as thin and regular as cotton thread. He touched the tip of his tongue to it and looked at her. How strange his eyes were, silver-grey. She suppressed a shiver. Through the blue-black square of the skylight, she saw the pole star.

'Yep,' he said, bitter. 'The sky's still the sky. Even round here.'

The rink was scruffy, vast, stained. Young people shouted and pushed one another in a slapstick film where nothing hurt.

Sarah took off her shoes and stood at the ladies' hatch, water soaking her socks. She pressed her feet into rigid boots and they snapped shut, squeezing down on her instep.

A chill rose. Johnny wasn't out yet. She tottered to a gap in the barrier and, gripping it with both hands, edged on. The ice was outrageously slippery.

In tiny steps she made her way around. It took courage to cross the next gap and she leant over the barrier to take the strain off her back. You never forget how to ride a bike, they say, but it seems you forget how to skate.

Behind her, a lad staggered sideways. 'Watch out, love,' one of his mates yelled. 'He's out of control!'

Johnny staggered across the ice towards her, arms flailing.

'I'll take you round,' he said. 'If you like.'

'Is that a good idea?' she asked.

He shrugged.

She gripped his arm and they advanced a couple of paces.

'It's not gonna work,' he said. 'Not if you cling to the side like that.'

She looked down at the blue-white surface, churned and re-frozen into icy rubble.

'C'mon,' he said. 'It'll be easier in the middle. The ice'll be smoother.'

She glanced to where other, braver people sailed.

'Stop looking at your feet!' She raised her eyes and it made her wobble. 'Let go of the barrier, will you,' he said. Clenching every muscle, she let go. He started towing her towards the centre. The ice moved under her feet.

'Your legs are far too stiff,' he said. 'Bend your knees. C'mon! Relax! You're making it hard work for both of us.'

Sarah imagined falling; her hand sliced by a blade. The side got further away.

'Slow down!' she shouted, not daring to move her head to look at him.

'Like there's a speed limit,' he said.

She tried to laugh.

At Akbar's, he seemed impatient while she studied the menu, and she ordered something she didn't really like. They nibbled raw onion dipped in mint raita, fractured a poppadom and poked its spikes into mango chutney and lime pickle. They drank lager from a corner-shop four pack. The main courses arrived, yellow and orange. Sarah ate slowly. She'd got round the rink without falling but her back was killing her. She reached for another beer.

'Should you be having that?' he asked.

'Two beers won't take me over the limit.'

She'd hoped they might talk houses, pasts, families, but it was like trying to start a car with a flat battery. Johnny grunted when she talked about her new start up North and didn't talk back. In the silence of their table, she was conscious of animated conversations at other tables. One group was having a particularly good time. Work colleagues, perhaps. She liked her co-workers at the hospital. Early days, though.

'Have you ever driven?' she asked.

'Only a windsurf board,' he said.

'Can't be much call for those in the city.'

'There's a couple of decent reservoirs on the outskirts. The wind speed gets up to about twenty-five knots. I've planed on the water at that speed before now.'

It was the most he'd said all evening.

The only parking space was right outside his house, spotlit by a yellow streetlamp. She stopped the car in the middle of the road. 'Thanks for a lovely evening.'

Lovely wasn't right. But she had no word for what it had been.

'Coffee?' he said.

They'd had coffee in the curry house. Or rather she had, while he ate mango kulfi. She'd rehearsed what she'd say if this moment came. Thanks, but no thanks. I'm on standby all this week.

'Okay,' she said.

There was no coffee. On the way upstairs, he collected a CD player and in the attic, he put some trance stuff on. She hoped he wasn't going to produce dope or mushrooms. She would have to draw the line at that. She sat on a floor cushion, holding a yellow stone to her cheek, trying to absorb its coolness. He was going round the room with a lit match. Light glowed through wax.

He snuffed the match and came to sit beside her.

Her mouth was dry. 'Lovely music. What is it?'

His eyes, pale and mirror-like in the candlelight, seemed to say that words were an evasion. She couldn't help uttering a few more. 'Sorry. I'm a bit nervous. I don't usually do this kind of thing.'

'What kind of thing?'

Her laugh sounded hysterical. 'Whatever it is we're doing.'

'Fucking,' he said, and pushed her back on the cushion.

She woke to a persistent bleep and pale clusters bathed in shafts of light. For a moment, she thought she was on the sea bed and fought for air. Then she saw Johnny, lying on his front, his head turned away.

She reached for her trousers, inside out with the knickers on top.

Her body felt as if they were still doing it, the hairs on his legs tickling the backs of hers. Her knees were sore and she tingled and throbbed. Some of the positions had been uncomfortable without a bed. She wouldn't have done them, normally. But last night, he'd taken her to a point where she'd have done almost anything. It had felt like drowning. She ought to think about that, perhaps. But not now. She fished in her trouser pocket for her pager.

The number wasn't one she recognised. They always called you at three in the morning. Last time it had been a burst pipe.

She lay back on the sleeping mat, toying with the idea of not ringing back. She saw the pole star again. On Bonfire Nights, her father had used to point out the constellations: Orion's three-starred belt, the smear of glitter that was the Seven Sisters. She gazed at Johnny, naked in the moonlight, his arms tucked in at his sides. Perhaps if she went now, she could be back before he woke. Did he work? She didn't know.

She crept out from under the unzipped sleeping bag and dressed quietly. She went round to his side, thinking she'd kiss his cheek. When she saw his face, she started back. His eyes were only half shut. She barely breathed as she waited for him to speak. But a snore showed he was asleep.

Downstairs, before she made the phone call, she opened cupboard doors, hoping to find coffee or tea bags. She found lidless pans and in the fridge, a drum of fish oil capsules.

Nothing was moving in the city centre except the traffic lights, playing their red, amber and green show to an empty theatre.

Sarah parked right outside the hospital, impossible in daytime, and hurried to the ward. Mustard walls and strip lights that might have been on forever. She went up in the lift. In her handbag, Johnny's door keys chinked against hers.

On the ward, the lights were low but patients were awake, murmuring and calling. A nurse passed from one bed bay to another. Another woman in dark blue walked an elderly man down the corridor. She nodded at Sarah. 'They know what's occurred. It upsets them.'

'I might have to call in an outside service. Is there money in the ward budget?'

'Absolutely not,' said the sister, opening the toilet door and manoeuvring the man through. 'It should come out of the property and support services budget. Your department.'

'Does the hospital have an account with anyone?'

The toilet door closed.

'Thanks a lot,' said Sarah. It was no good asking the nurse she'd seen earlier. When the door opened again, she followed the sister and the old man down the corridor. 'I take it you've tried the – you know.'

'There'd be no-one there at this time of night,' snapped the sister.

'The porters' lodge?'

'Hardly relevant if there's nowhere to porter it to.'

The sister steered her patient into bed. 'Look, it's come on top of the one we were expecting,' she said as she lifted his feet.

'We've space reserved for one, but not two.'

'You can't leave it in the bed till morning?'

'You must be joking. The relatives are here. They're starting to make noises.'

Several funeral directors offered a twenty four hour service. To get the job done, Sarah paid for the private ambulance with her credit card. It wasn't what you were meant to do but the clock above the ward clerk's desk said nearly four thirty and the sister and the nurse had disappeared. She scribbled a note to the sister, grabbed her bag and headed for the exit.

In the depths of a bed bay, a face turned, an arm waved.

She glanced down the corridor. No staff in sight.

'Fuck's sake.' She entered the dark bay, hastened past the mounds in the other beds.

The patient's face was gaunt, his legs low ridges in the sheet. Plastic tubes attached him to various bags. Fluids going in, coming out.

'I'm not a nurse,' she said. 'I'm admin. I'll fetch someone.'

He pawed her arm. He looked like the one who'd been helped to the toilet. 'I heard him, nurse,' he said, urgent. Upper teeth gleamed grey in the dark. 'I heard what he said before he went.'

Without wanting to, she looked across the bay to a curtained bed. A bedside light was on inside: the whole oblong glowed like a huge candle. That must be where the corpse lay.

'We only knew each other a few days,' said the man. He spoke in a thick whisper. 'But you get real close in here. It's like soldiers. You...'

A middle-aged man in a dark suit slipped out from behind the lit curtains. The old man raised his hand in a half wave that went unseen.

'That's his son,' he whispered as the younger man left the bay. He strained up from the pillow, trying to see where the son had gone.

'His daughter's been called.' He spoke as though he had hopes of the daughter. 'I haven't got sons. I haven't got daughters. But it was me as heard him at the last.'

She leant towards him, steeling herself for a revelation: a crime committed years ago; a family secret; an indictment of one of the doctors.

He elbowed himself to a sit, waving away her pillow arranging skills. He motioned her close. He spoke with vinegar breath. 'He told me, "I'm not going home again, am I? I'm never going back to my flat."'

They looked at each other. 'He said it more 'n once,' said the man. 'I reckon when they didn't answer, that was when he knew.'

He gave himself back to his pillows. Sarah felt empty, as if something had been taken from her. She glanced around his meagre territory. A plastic chair stood by the bed. A locker bore a get-well card, a jug of water, a blister pack of kiwi fruit.

She wanted to tell him it would be different for him; he would get better and go back to wherever he called home, where china shepherdesses stood equally spaced on the mantelpiece, perhaps, or books and CDs rose in dizzy piles from the floor. She wanted to tell him that he would drink tea from his own mug; pop two slices of white bread into his own toaster.

Instead, she lowered herself into the plastic chair and thought of her own living room, with its brown corduroy sofa covered in cat hairs; its glass door panes that cast blue and red jewels of light; its flames painted on hardboard and propped against the unused fireplace. It was home, now.

The sister, passing the bay, nodded to her. She gazed at the glowing curtains opposite. She would go in a minute. But as the old man began to snore, she sat on.

Unaccustomed

At break behind the toilet block, Omo makes me learn a new clapping game.

'One meter, two meter, three meter,' she chants. The vulture watches from above, hunched in its black cloak.

'Faster, faster,' says Omo. If I lose, I get a Chinese burn. If I win, I can wear her silver ring for a count of one hundred. I've had a Chinese burn before, but not a ring. My mother says it's vulgar for young girls to wear jewellery, that it makes them grow up too soon. Her rings are gold, one plain and one with stones in a row. I tried them on when she was asleep once, and the turquoise jewels slid round, became secret in my palm.

When the bell goes for end of break, Omo tells me I've won but doesn't say why. She gives me her ring, starts counting again. I put it on my thumb because that's where she wears it. My hands are brown for an *oyinbo*, but they'll never be brown as hers. The ring looks pretty. It fits me well.

She speeds up her counting. She grabs my wrist and twists the ring off my thumb.

'Ow.'

'It's your own fault,' she says.

'It's not. Can I wear it again?'

'Maybe, maybe not.'

We have English next. We are both in the top tier. Afterwards I'm going home with her for lunch. It will be the first time I've been in a proper Nigerian house. My mother told me to wash my hands, but she didn't say whether I should do it before or after.

The vulture's head is red, like meat. I do a big shudder.

'*Chei!*' says Omo. 'That bird is not interested in us. It is interested in dead things. How many times I got to tell you?'

The principal is called Sister Jacinta. She's tiny and plump, and last week she called my mother in and sat us in front of her desk. The fan rattled and wobbled until I thought it would fall off.

'How,' Sister asked my mother, 'is your daughter getting on? Is she settling in?'

My mother's lips went tight. She had wiped her red lipstick off before we went in, but there was some left in the corners.

'Are her marks not good, Sister?' she asked.

'Her marks are fine,' said the principal. 'More than fine. My only concern is whether she's finding her feet. Among her classmates.'

'Well, of course she is,' said my mother, very certain. She was always very certain when she didn't know.

The principal talked some more. Norms, she said. Differences. Unaccustomed. She talked so much that my mother had time to go all the way from annoyed to tired. And then the principal stood up and said she was sure it would all come out in the wash but that she felt easier in her heart now that she and my mother had been able to have this little chat. And that was that. I stared at her.

My mother did a little curtsey when they shook hands but outside in the shade of the school trees, she pulled my arm back and slapped me on the back of the legs. I looked at the principal's window, hoping she'd seen and would come running out and arrest my mother for beating me. But the school building remained sleepy and still.

'What was all that about?' my mother asked. 'I haven't got time for this, on top of everything else.'

'What's everything else?' I asked, anxious.

My mother sighed. 'Nothing,' she said. 'What's going on?'

'Nothing,' I said.

My mother's eyes went into slits. 'I'm not going to ask you again.'

I shrugged.

'Are you being bullied?' asked my mother. 'Is that what she was hinting at?'

She made it sound as if whatever the thing was, it was my fault. She always did that. I shook my head.

'Because if you are, you should tell me and your father,' said my mother. 'Then we can do something about it.'

Sometimes, she has no idea.

We left the shade of the school trees and walked out onto the Ikot Ekpene Road.

'This damn heat,' she said. 'It'll finish us all off.'

I shrugged.

'As for you, you'll end up behind a counter in Woolworth's if you're not careful,' she said.

It was hard to picture Woolworth's. It was months since I'd been there. But I remembered a Mr Softy ice cream machine and jewellery that glittered under glass. 'Yes please,' I said.

Omo lives in a house called a face-me-I-slap-you. The house opposite is so close, the neighbours can see into her family's front room. They know if she skips breakfast, Omo says. She hears their tongues click when she goes to bed late.

I'm surprised by how dark it is inside and how small the

windows are. Children and grownups are crammed round a long table and there's no room for anything else, even air. We stand by the door.

'This my class mate Zara,' says Omo.

They stop talking and the children stare. 'Welcome. How you dey, Zara?' says the man at the head of the table. His beard is like white dust.

'I am well. Thank you very much for asking,' I say.

The children giggle. 'Come chop, baby,' says a boy and pushes the boy next to him off the end of the bench. Everyone laughs.

I don't want to sit next to a boy but I don't want to be rude either, so I just stand there. I look to Omo but she laughs. Then a girl in a pink dress makes room for me.

My sides get hot, pressed between people. I tell myself not to faint. I fainted when I was six, outside the butcher's in Gloucester. When I came round I was lying on a freezing cold pavement and the butcher was pushing snuff up my nose.

A woman dishes out food. She is wearing a piece of yellow material as a dress. 'One, one, one,' she says as she passes the plates. The man says, 'as I taste, so they should taste; as I swallow, so they should swallow.' He must be Omo's father. I sneak a look at his leg, in his shorts, but I can't see the bullet wound he's supposed to have. It stops him working, Omo says, so he sits around the house all day criticising everyone.

Everyone starts eating without waiting for their knives and forks. Then I realise there are no knives and forks. Omo digs me with her elbow. 'Like this,' she says loudly, so that everyone can hear. She takes a pinch of rice and puts it in her mouth. The woman in yellow frowns at her.

My mother says that eating with your fingers is unsanitary.

I look around. Everyone has their elbows on the table. They are eating and talking at the same time. Their fingers shine with red grease. I was hungry before but my appetite has gone. I shake my head.

'*Chei*,' says Omo and makes a big thing out of tipping my rice onto her plate.

When all the food has been eaten, the younger boys are allowed to get down from the table. They run outside and I hear their ball bouncing away down the alley.

'You girls gon stir yourselves?' asks the woman. 'Gon help me clear these dishes and serve the fruit?'

I know Omo won't help because she thinks children shouldn't be made to wash up. Also, she likes coconut candy for pudding, not fruit. So I get down to start helping. The woman frowns again. 'Not you, pikin,' she says. The girl in the pink dress gets down and starts collecting plates. The men sit back and pick their teeth.

The man with the pearly beard speaks to Omo, and the woman goes out and comes back with something wrapped in a banana leaf. She gives it to Omo and suddenly we are not getting any fruit but are outside, walking past some houses painted bright green.

I'm glad I managed to say that the meal was lovely before we left, even though Omo glared at me when I did.

We cross some wasteland and get back onto the Ikot Ekpene Road. There are hardly any cars but there are always boys on mopeds who think it is fun to run you over, so we walk on the grass at the edge. I could never walk in bare feet the way Omo does.

'Are we going back to school?' I ask Omo.

'You will see,' she says.

She never tells me anything.

Her green parcel is coming apart.

'Haven't you heard of Tupperware?' I ask.

'Everyone has heard of Tupperware.' The pearls in her ears go right through like staples. I wish I had pearls but there's no point in asking. My mother's pearls are clip-ons and they pinch so hard that your ear nearly drops off. But she says it's the kind of pain you get used to, that after a while you stop noticing.

'So, what *is* Tupperware?' I ask.

'Don't you know?'

I kick at a clump of grass. 'Of course.'

'So tell me.'

'I asked you first.'

She doesn't reply. We walk for a bit. It's very hot and there's no shade unless you are a *lekpa shandy* and can hide behind a telegraph pole. The poles shimmer off in a long line like mirages.

'Who were all those people in your house?' I ask. 'They can't *all* be your family.'

I think about my mother and father and my cousins who are both boys. I often wish I had a sister.

Omo pulls a face. 'They been coming round since I was born,' she says. 'Since before I was born.'

We get to the school but we walk right past so we must be going into town. We turn left and right until the market is in front of us.

The market is huge and always crowded. I've been past in the car but I've never been in. I walk slower. I don't like people staring and trying to touch my hair. My father does most of our shopping. He drives to Kingsway in Port Harcourt in the company Land Rover and sometimes I'm allowed to go with him. It's clean in Kingsway, and cool from the freezer cabinets. You can forget you live in Africa.

'What's the matter?' asks Omo. 'The fear catch you?'

'Course not,' I say and walk faster. I have to pretend I'm fine, because she makes up names for people. She called me Pee Pee Leg for weeks.

Vegetables are heaped on the ground. A woman lies on a pile of potatoes. Another woman scoops milk out of a drum, pours it into a plastic bag and holds it out to me. She smiles but she has no teeth. I don't recognise half the food people are selling, under umbrellas and sheets of plastic. Bike bells ring and people shout. A boy pushes a pillar of plastic buckets over and runs away laughing.

We come to a building with a roof made of tin sheets and we go in. Inside it smells of metal. The walls are dark and the tables go up and down. I see black stuff sliding in a tray; grey rubber coils rising in a pile. I move closer. I forget to pretend. 'What are those?'

'They are peeled snakes,' says Omo. Her voice is soft.

I jump back.

'They're dead, *mumu*,' she says. 'They can't bite you now.'

I try to un-think snake. I look at the other tables. Slabs and chunks loll, pink piles slither. Meat hangs off edges like old dishcloths.

I catch my breath.

'Zara,' says Omo. 'How come you afraid of each and every little thing?'

A pig goes past on a man's shoulder, bristly and black. Its dead eyes stare at me. I wish everything didn't stare.

I stand there, wondering how far our house in Fuel Plantation is, and whether I could run all the way back without stopping.

Then a word comes to me, and, by the way it prickles my brain, I know it's a magic word.

'I'm not afraid,' I say. 'I'm just… unaccustomed.'

'Onna-what?' asks Omo.

'Unaccustomed. It means not being used to things.'

Omo smiles. She loves new words. 'On-na-cos-stom,' she says, and goes on saying it as we walk towards the bright oblong at the other end of the hall, forgetting that she is meant to be teasing me.

We come out at the place where people throw things out in buckets. The mud is full of blood and other things I don't want to think about, but I try not to worry about my shoes or what anyone will say about them later.

Omo walks up to a big umbrella where a girl stands next to some pots on a wide brazier. She knocks fists with the girl, the way boys do.

I stand at the edge. The girl looks over to me. She is tall and wears a purple headscarf. She looks like Omo.

'Ndewo,' she says. 'So, you are Zara. My sister tell me all about you.'

I don't know whether this is good or bad.

She holds her hand out for a proper handshake. There is a bad blister on her hand and I hesitate.

'Don't worry,' she says. 'It is not catching. I am Grace.'

'Very pleased to meet you,' I say, and she laughs.

Omo hands over the banana leaf parcel and Grace opens it. '*Chei*, cold jollof rice,' she says, and puts it to one side.

She turns and fishes something out of a pot that looks like string. She throws it into a frying pan where it hisses and smokes. She flips it in the pan. By her brazier is a tub of red dust and a bucket of yellowy white slabs. I stand on tiptoe to see everything.

'Take a closer look,' says Grace. 'The fat don't bite. The spice don't bite. '

I go to the brazier. In the pot, dirty foam trembles. It smells bad.

'This is my snack,' the sister says. 'When they give me a break from school, I come back to Aba and boil and fry for the market women.'

'Yeah,' says Omo. 'The men won't eat it.'

'It is too good for them,' says Grace, and they laugh.

'You want try?' she asks me, scooping a piece up with her spatula and holding it out. The fat twinkles, then is still. They watch as I pick it up with the tips of my nails and nibble the end. The snack makes my lips tingle. Omo's eyes dance. Before she can accuse me of being scared, I shove the whole thing into my mouth.

At first it's fine. then my mouth catches fire. I gasp and turn to Omo, but she is bent over, laughing. I open my mouth and try to fan air in. My nose starts running. Sneezes come one after the other. Tears run down my cheeks. My eyes sting so much I can't open them any more. I could spit it out, I think, but I don't want to be rude, so I swallow it instead. I start coughing. I bend over. I cough and I cough. I have to hold the tops of my legs.

'Zara, Zara! You are okay?' Grace's voice. 'My snack is too spicy, na so?'

I try to speak. 'The snack was lovely,' I squeak. 'Thank you very much.'

I hear laughter, then someone grabs my hand. It must be Omo. I can't open my eyes to see.

'I'm not crying,' I tell her. 'It's just water coming out of my tear ducts.'

'Tear ducks?' says Omo. 'What is tear ducks?'

But another sneeze is building and I can't tell her.

I feel her twist something onto my thumb. I recognise the feeling of her ring. I make a noise like a dog barking. As soon as I can speak, I'm going to ask Grace for another piece.

The Unified Medical Dictionary

'You seem out of breath,' says your mother, as she tucks the mosquito net in around your bed. 'I've told you not to run on a full stomach.'

You nod. You're hoping she won't look under the bed. As a decoy, you pick up your doll and stroke its long orange hair.

Your mother smiles. 'I was beginning to think you'd lost interest in poor old Rita.'

When she's gone, you throw the doll down the bed. Its head hits the footboard and it falls down between the net and mattress and hangs there looking surprised.

The murmur of their voices comes through the bedroom wall. Like you, they always have an afternoon nap but you're the only one who has to stay in bed for a whole hour.

You turn to the window. The net makes a milky cocoon but when you put your face close to it, it vanishes.

At the end of the compound is a concrete block with two squares for windows. A garden fork is stabbed into the ground and the servants' monkey lives on the handle. It spends hours turning a teaspoon over and over in its hands, which are like tiny leather gloves.

This time yesterday, Chidike came out and squatted by the ants' nest with a kettle. The nest is only a small red heap but everyone says it has to be stopped. When he poured the water, the ants boiled up out of the eye of the nest. It made you jump back from the window. But he stayed still and let them run over his feet and ankles. You watched, and the net grew damp where your mouth was.

Your father falls asleep quickly – you have to give him that. He's a scientist and even his snores are important. You certainly aren't allowed to complain about them, anyway.

You untuck the net on one side and climb out. You slide a big navy cube out from under the bed.

Archimedes, the greatest mathematician of antiquity, invented the Law of the Lever in 250 BC so that people could move heavy things by tipping them. It was thanks to this principle that you were able to get the book up the stairs, though you dragged it across the landing without any principle at all.

The book has metal corners, cool and smooth. You open it near the beginning. A scent of toast wafts up from the pages, which are crammed with more words than you've ever seen. *Adenoids,* you read. Your cousin has adenoids. You read the description. *Lymphoid tissue that forms a prominence on the wall of the nasopharynx.*

You frown and try *bilharzia,* a disease that Roy Davies, a man at your father's work, has got. *Schistosome,* you read, *trematode worm parasite.* You know what a worm is. But then *miracidia, urinary tract.*

You sit back. You're supposed to be a good reader.

Perhaps you'll try *haemorrhage.* Last month, when your mother stayed in bed for three days, the doctor from Port Harcourt said *haemorrhage.* You asked what it meant. But no-one replied and your father said, don't go upsetting her all over again. He said it was reprehensible. *Reprehensible.* So then there were two words you didn't understand.

You decide to go straight to the colour plates.

They lie in the centre of the book in a blue-white stripe, each one separated by tracing paper. You've seen your father looking at them and it has made you curious.

The first picture is a sort of tongue with a stick inside. *Portal vein*, says grey labelling. *Hepatic artery. Orifice of common bile-duct.* You run your finger around the outline of the tongue, first one way then the other.

Next is a hand, wearing a glove sewn all over with pretty pink and yellow embroidery. *Transverse fasciculi. Palmar aponeurosis.*

When the girls at school like something, they say it's standard. As you go on through the colour plates, you decide that every single one is standard. There's a thing like a centipede rearing up: *the spine. The ear* is a weird snail. Then comes a walnut, except it's called *the brain*.

The final plate is a foldout. You hesitate because if it's a foldout, it probably contains something major. Your father's snore is still there, drowning out the whir of the fridge downstairs and the beat of the ceiling fan on the landing.

You unfold the plate. A man and a woman stand next to each other. They are very life-like. And they are in the nude. The woman has bosoms. But it's the man your eyes fly to.

You've seen your cousin's. He showed you in the bathroom back in England, and you pulled your own pants down in return. He said you did it too quick and he didn't see anything. Then he cried but you laughed because you knew he couldn't tell his mother why. You didn't see much either, though you pretended you had.

But here, amid black hairy triangles, you can see everything. *Vas deferens*, you read. You forget to breathe. *Testis. Seminal vesicle.*

You take it all in: the tunnels and chambers, the spirals, the holes, the pockets and pipes. You read all the labels. *Glans. Corpus cavernosum. Corpus spongiosum.* You imagine showing Omo and the other girls at school. How they would clutch their little silver crosses and fan themselves!

It's easier getting the book down the stairs than it was getting it up. At the bottom, you fetch a roller skate from a cupboard and manoeuvre the book onto it.

The wheel and axle principle was invented by the Sumerians, who entered Mesopotamia in 4,000 BC. They were the first people to divide space and time into units of six, and were as clever as Modern Man. The only thing was, they didn't say much about steering. The book veers into the kitchen and bashes into the screen door and when you push it down the compound, it travels in a wild zigzag.

Outside the hut, two tin plates bake in the sun. The door, a bead curtain, leaks voices.

You stop and glance back at the shutters of the main house. Nothing has ever been said, but the hut is probably out of bounds. You know Chidike but the cook is new. He is from a different tribe and hardly ever speaks.

But you can't stand here all day getting sunstroke. Holding your breath in case there's a smell, you push the skate through the curtain.

It's so dark you can't see a thing. And it has gone quiet, like a radio being turned off.

Then Chidike speaks. 'That's some book, pikin.'

You have to work your eyes. Shapes appear; a mattress in the corner, the two men sitting on the floor. They aren't wearing their regulation red check shirts. A scar like a dark string with knots runs across the cook's back. And as you feared, there is a smell. It's like stewed apple.

But this is about Science. You push the skate into the middle. The wheels go over some playing cards, but you can't help that. You open the book, unfold the last colour plate and stand back.

Distant guns sometimes go off in the night and the silence afterwards goes on forever. It's like that now. Then the cook clicks his tongue, gets up and walks to the door.

Chidike says something.

'Speak in English, please,' you say.

But he goes on talking in his own language. Then he laughs, and his teeth shine.

The cook just stands in the doorway, shaking his head.

All in all, it is disappointing. You think you might as well sit down. More things have appeared in the room: the red check shirts, hanging on a hat stand; the dark coil of a millipede in a corner. Forks stand next to cups on a table with two rolled mats underneath.

Your mother says there aren't enough things out here for a self-respecting family. Judging by the hut, the servants have even fewer things. That's good, you decide: it means less tidying up.

A deck of cards lies face down. You recognise bare bosoms again, and are edging closer when a sound like rain makes you look round.

A stone forms in your throat. Your father stands blinking in the doorway, the beads of the curtain jumping around him.

'See trouble,' hisses the cook.

Before you hide your face in your knees, you see that the book is now somehow closed, the colour plate shovelled back in.

You hear the cook say the master is a good master and he wants no trouble with such a master. You hear Chidike say the master's daughter is a clever girl who is teaching the servants best grammar. Then your arm burns and beads sting your face. Outside everything is white.

Your father marches you across the compound and throws you into a chair at the dining table. Your knee is singing. The book lands in front of you, its cover scratched and damaged.

But that's the least of your worries.

'What did you show them?' His voice is full of spit.

'Nothing.'

You brace yourself for a slap.

He flips the cover open so hard it bounces.

'Show me. Show me what you showed them.'

Your hands jump onto the pages and begin turning them.

Artery, Babinski sign, cataract. Dengue fever, earache, falciparum malaria. The meanings skip away, even of the things you thought you knew.

Gallbladder, hepatitis, injections. The weight of the turned pages makes the book creep to the left. The middle approaches. *Jaundice, Kaposi's sarcoma, leprosy, miscarriage.*

You touch the first tracing paper leaf.

'One by one,' says your father.

You have no plan. You are already going as slow as you dare. The first diagram is the tongue thing. Your eyes skid over it.

You turn to the embroidered hand. The spine. The eyeball. *Retina. Lacrima caruncle. Vitreous gel.*

You are getting near the fold out. You pray for it to be gone, for the servants to have done a juju on it. When you see it under the next tracing paper leaf, you feel sick.

You feel your father's heat at your back.

You want the hut with the cups and forks, the millipede in the corner. You want your doll, your room, the quiet hour you once thought boring.

They say understanding comes like a light bulb, though it couldn't have for Archimedes and the Sumerians because light bulbs weren't invented then. They were invented by Thomas Eddison in 1879.

But suddenly you are no longer afraid. You can't even remember why you were afraid. You know for certain that your father saw nothing in the hut and is relying on you to give yourself away.

You unfold the plate with great care.

They are all still there; the triangles of black hair, the hanging pouch, the big thingy.

But you move your eyes across them as if they were nothing.

Then you start on the woman. *Uterus, vagina. Clitoris.*

You turn the page. You are careful not to sigh. You continue with the same care through *neurosurgery, onanism, Paget's disease, quarantine* and *rectum.* At *skeleton,* you breathe out. *Tricuspid valve, urine, Voluntary Euthanasia Society, wrist, X-ray.* At *yellow fever* you clear your throat. The last entry is *zygotic lethal gene.* You close the book.

'Again,' says your father. 'We'll sit here all day if we have to.'

You go through the book again. This time when the colour plates arrive, you linger on *the stomach* and say, 'Mm.'

You want to laugh at your own daring.

You are starting for a third time when your mother's voice makes you look up.

'Are you nearly done, Jim? Sarah needs to finish her nap and

I need the table for some sewing.'

Your father hesitates. Then he sighs and stands up and slides the book off the table. It goes back on the shelf but only just. The other books must have breathed out while it was away.

You look at your mother. She motions you towards the stairs. You need no second bidding.

It's wonderful to be back in your room. On the bed, you rescue Rita, straighten her dress and prop her on the pillow, where she sits holding out her arms. You hum as you try and tuck the net back in around the two of you. But it's impossible to do, from the inside.

Three for the Price of Five

You don't want to go. But you have to, and not just because of your mother.

Inside, it's old and dusty and four rows of hard chairs stand in a semi-circle. You're in school uniform. In the toilet, you fling talcum powder up your skirt to stop the tops of your thighs stinging where they've rubbed. You head for the back row, for a seat behind a black woman called Wanda. You sit in the lavender stink of the talcum. It has smeared your shoes. Wanda's back shelters you as you examine your split ends.

The lecture begins. The leader keeps saying the word substitute. You glance around to see if anyone else finds it funny but they seem to be hanging on her every word. You can't concentrate. You chew skin off the side of your thumb. It was red even when you started but you can't stop. You gaze at dust motes, floating weightless in the fans of light cast down from the high windows.

Your mother has photos of a girl who stands in an African compound, holding a bottle of orange Fanta (not the diet kind) to the black stitched snout of a Teddy. Now you're nearly a teenager, and Teddy's eyes have loosened; become deranged.

The leader calls Wanda up. Wanda's chair makes a splintering sound as she stands. She takes her time getting to the front, despite the leader's apologetic glances to the others. When the leader makes her announcement, Wanda says 'badderation' and winks at you. Then she ambles back.

It's your turn. You have to stand on white rubber footprints to make sure the reading is accurate. Standing on one leg or leaning back is forbidden. Your feet overlap the prints. Girls' shoes never fit you and you end up wearing boys' ones.

'Oh dear,' the leader whispers. Your reading is worse than expected. Ladies murmur, perhaps in sympathy, perhaps in disgust. You see again the actions of your week, actions you described to yourself at the time as misdemeanours. Because you didn't get away with it, they now seem like capital offences.

Using your hair as a curtain, you walk back to your seat. Wanda turns. 'Don' worry child,' she whispers, 'dem scales is prably rang.'

But you have gone over the eleven stone barrier, which means your father will be told. He'll subject you to a tongue-lashing. Or he'll laugh and your mother will scream that everything goes to pot when the sun goes over the yardarm.

You decide to lie. It won't really be a lie, because you will make up for it. Tomorrow is Friday, a good day for a fresh start.

You slip out of the church hall, trying not to activate the floorboards. With a fresh start in the offing, it doesn't matter what happens now. Today is a write-off anyway.

You set off for the High Street, where you buy five jam doughnuts for the price of three.

You love doughnuts. They are squishy, like babies. When your mother was in hospital, you stayed at your friend's for a week and got treats in your packed lunch every day. Doughnuts, Cheesy Wotsits, fairy cakes – home baked! – with silver balls, peanut butter sandwiches, mini pork pies with their pink, private insides: all the things you aren't allowed to eat normally, packed in a blue box with a lid that clicked shut. It was your treasure chest.

You eat them as slowly as you can on the way back to the church hall, holding the paper bag close to your mouth. The doors leak music and thumping. There are two doughnuts left and you contemplate life's saddest truth: however hungry you are to start with, the more you eat, the more the pleasure of eating diminishes.

You take a bite from the penultimate doughnut. But here, parked beyond the gravestones, is your mother's car. It is a brown Hillman Imp. She is staring out of the window right at you. You release the doughnut immediately. It drops into the bag and you swallow what's in your mouth, keeping your jaw rigid so it doesn't look like eating. Then you blow your nose on the bag as if it is a hanky and stuff it into your pocket. Nonchalant, you think.

But your mother has got out of the car. You long for the shops and buses of the High Street, where nobody knows you. A squirrel is transfixed at the base of a tree. The breeze presses its fur into rosettes.

'Mother,' you say as you reach her, 'you're early.'

'So this is what you've been doing,' she says. Her trembling mouth and hot eyes make you think suddenly of the mad woman in the attic, from *Jane Eyre*, that you've nearly finished reading. Is this what she looked like?

You look at the squirrel instead. It runs up the tree in stops and starts. In between, it's utterly still.

'Waiting until my back is turned,' hisses your mother. 'Get into the car, Sarah. Now.'

The squirrel shoots into the canopy and is gone.

One doughnut, squashed. One doughnut bitten into, its shining ruby well exposed. One crumpled paper bag, translucent. You flinch from the flagrant display on the dashboard.

'Turn your pockets inside out,' says your mother.

'They're empty,' you say.

She makes you do it anyway. In one pocket, jam has spread incontinent over the black lining. Both pockets bristle with old crumbs and fluff.

'How many have you already eaten?' she demands.

'One,' you say. 'I got three for the price of five.'

She can't prove otherwise, you think, chewing your thumb.

She says, 'Do you think I'm an idiot?'

'No,' you say.

'There's obviously something wrong with you, something very, very wrong.'

This is true and you have to try very hard not to cry, seeing your thumb that is red in some places and blubbery in others, your feet in their horrible brown boys' shoes, and your knees, fat and high next to your mother's. She is very slim and achieves it by monitoring every mouthful. Your father eats like a pig but she doesn't care about that. 'Yes, but Daddy isn't obese,' she says when you complain.

A tap on the window makes you jump.

The red feathers on Wanda's hat dance on long stalks. Your mother tuts and opens the window a crack. Wanda puts her mouth to the crack and aims her voice through it.

'You dis child's madda?' she asks. Your mother stares. 'Madame,' says Wanda, 'this child is a credit to you. She hap right an them scales rain or shine. She hole her head up whatever dat boasie woman in there say. She don' take it too serious, not like the rest a dem wanga-guts.'

She stands, her mouth an inch from the window. She seems to be waiting. But your mother's mouth is an 'O'. Wanda waits again then gives you a business-like nod. 'And she less than half de age of anyone else in de whole damn place,' she says, and moves off.

You look at your mother, your heart waiting for permission to beat again.

Your mother shakes her head. 'Good god, the size of that woman,' she says. 'She's really let herself go. What does she think she looks like? And in that ridiculous hat.' You burn with the injustice of this verdict. 'I suppose you've been telling tales about me,' says your mother.

You would like to point out that you never mention your mother to anyone, not to tell tales, not to tell anything.

But your mother is calming down and you don't want to jeopardize it. Soon she will move to stage two, injury and pleading. It's bad but not as bad as stage one.

Your mother sighs. 'Whatever you may think, she says, I am not doing this for my own benefit. I'm doing it to help you.'

Wanda is crossing the road, unhurried, an ocean liner pulling out of dock. 'Willpower is the only answer,' your mother is saying, 'but you have got to want to help yourself. I can't do it for you, I wish I could.'

It is a song that has been at Number One longer than 'Bridge Over Troubled Water' by Simon and Garfunkel.

At home, you have four sanctuaries. A fruit cake wrapped in foil from someone's wedding matures in the sideboard. From its flat base you regularly shave thin, complete discs. Chocolate biscuits, your parents' Saturday morning treat, stand in columns in the spare room wardrobe, behind a pile of blankets. You eat whole packs in one go. In the chest freezer in the garage, bread rolls, hard and cold, lie swaddled in cloudy plastic. No-one counts them. Sometimes you don't bother to defrost them first.

In the shoebox under your bed, Nana's old letters cover a family bar of fruit and nut. You imagine breaking huge diagonal chunks from it, putting the rows of hard squares in your mouth, feeling the edges melt.

Your mother puts the car into gear and moves off.

She was fat as a girl, she told you once, and wants better for you. She wants you to meet a nice man, a doctor or an airline pilot. Or a teacher, as long as he treats you right. She wants you to settle down and be happy; to be loved and cherished. But it will never happen, she said, if you go on like this. She cried then you cried. She hugged you and you clung to her and promised to do better.

But you just can't do it. At school, you have turned it into a joke; drawn a pierced heart on your desk with your name on one side, chocolate on the other. But you don't really love food. If anything, you're scared of it.

You reach the High Street. Everything in Ann Summers' window is red and black. The colours of sex, you suppose, not that you will ever find out. Next door is the cake shop where you bought the doughnuts.

You give a little gasp. You can't help it. Coming out of the doughnut shop is Wanda, the feathers of her red hat trembling. Her bearing is military. You've never seen her smile, though one time she laughed and couldn't stop and the leader said funny as it no doubt was it was time to move on with the meeting.

She doesn't see you. But from the passenger seat of your mother's Hillman Imp, you give her your best secret wave, the one where only your fingers move and the rest of you stays utterly still.

Seed

From the back seat of the old Chevrolet, Sarah watched her father go round the house in the dark, rattling the shutters on the windows. Her mother sat silent in the passenger seat and the car headlights lit up a wedge of the garden, turning the aloe bushes to blazes of white fire.

They looked like spirit bushes.

'Does Chidike know we won't be here tomorrow?' Sarah asked.

The vinyl seat, red hot in the daytime, was cool against her legs.

'What?' said the mother, as if she'd never heard of Chidike, or tomorrow. Three days ago, the doctor at the hospital in Port Harcourt had given her something to help her sleep. But now she seemed to be asleep even when she was awake.

'He might be worried if I'm not there to help him in the compound,' said Sarah. 'The hen might not eat her seed.'

Her mother sighed. She obviously had no idea how skittish the hen was since the monkey had died. 'Sometimes I think you care about those servants more than you care about us,' she said. 'And at a time like this.'

But what sort of time was it? Sarah was too scared to ask. Questions bumped in her head like bugs trapped in a porch light.

Her father's knees appeared in the beam of the headlights. He slid into the driver's seat and the car began crawling over the track that led to the Ikot Ekpene Road. The beam danced and he did not make his usual joke about how the suspension was killing him.

Sarah took a last look at the aloe bushes. Sometimes Chidike made tiny goblets and swords from the silver paper that came with his Marlboros and left them under the aloe bushes for her to find. She hoped there weren't any there now. He might think she didn't care.

The journey lasted forever. Somewhere in the middle, they changed planes at an airport where sand stretched for miles beyond the plate glass windows. In the transfer lounge, among acres of shiny red sofas, a man with a tea towel on his head put his face close to Sarah's, opened his mouth and pointed. Gold teeth gleamed. She didn't know what he was trying to show her and no-one told him to go away. By the time the London flight was announced, her cheeks ached from pretend smiling.

When they boarded the coach at Victoria, it was midday.

'We're nearly home,' said her mother, and fell asleep with her head bumping against the window.

Sarah stared out at the pavements and roundabouts, the red buses and the white buildings. It didn't look like home. Everything was too close together, and there were too many people. The roads were too smooth. Her eyes, hot and dry, wouldn't close, as if someone had put a juju on them.

She suspected Joseph Adeola. He had brought a shrunken head to school last week. It was grey and creased, the size of a satsuma. Bits of hair hung down and the eyes and mouth were sewn up. It was from South America, he said. Some of the girls screamed. He said it was used as a cure. What for, the teacher had asked, headaches? Everyone laughed and the next day Joseph brought his uncle's finger to class, in a matchbox. The teacher said a bad word; the finger, crooked in the box, looked like a burnt chipolata sausage; Joseph rocked with mirth and banged his head on the desk.

They left the suburbs. Now everything was divided into fields, bright yellow and dark green, edged with stubby trees. Sarah thought of acacia trees, their canopies so tall that giraffes could stand under them without bending their necks. Chidike chewed on acacia twigs to clean his teeth. Perhaps giraffes did too.

Nana's house had a pimpled grey front and a fat green lawn. Normally, when you arrived on the doorstep, her snowy hair bobbed behind the oval pane before you could even knock. But today Sarah's father fished a key from his pocket.

In the hall, Nana's hexagonal mirror still hung on its chain but leaflets and newspapers swam on the doormat. Sarah glanced up the steep staircase, at the swirly pattern of blues and browns that sometimes appeared in her dreams. At the top was the indoor toilet her father had installed, but which Nana never used. She preferred the outside one, she'd whispered once, with its spiders and air. Sarah preferred the outside one too.

'Where is she?' asked Sarah.

Her mother let out a sob and her father took her mother's arm. Her mother pulled away and ran up the stairs. Her father followed, head low. Time passed.

Sarah stood in the hall, the suitcases flanking her like obedient dogs. Her legs ached but she didn't move.

The stairs squeaked as her father came down again and sat on the bottom step.

'Where's Nana?' asked Sarah again.

'She's gone to sleep,' said her father. A red curtain had appeared in his left eye, drawn halfway across.

Sarah concentrated on the other eye. 'So, can I just put my head round her door?' It was an expression her mother used.

'She's not in her room. She's... gone away.'

'Gone away where? Didn't she want to see us first?'

Her father studied his feet. 'Well yes of course she did. But in the end, it all happened in rather a rush.'

'A rush?'

'She couldn't wait. She'd come to the end of her time. Christ, why can't your mother be the one to speak to you about this?' Her father sighed. 'Look, she's gone to Heaven, love. 'To be with the angels.'

'You mean she's dead,' said Sarah.

Her father looked shocked. 'If you want to put it like that, yes.'

'So, has she gone to the waters under the earth?' asked Sarah.

Her father shook his head and stood up. His eye was the eye of a demon.

Sarah ran to Nana's back room. The dining table still stood against the far wall, the table Nana used for everything: shelling peas, reading the *Gloucester Citizen*, embroidering airmail paper with stories about going into town on the number nine and having cups of tea and buns at British Home Stores.

Sarah crawled under the fringe of its green chenille tablecloth. She hugged a heavy table leg, pressed herself into its hard spirals.

When she woke it was dark, and no-one had ordered her out or said only babies sat under tables. Something red and black growled and shifted in the grate. On the mantelpiece the carriage clock squatted next to the wooden mask they'd bought Nana at Christmas and which she said reminded her of a boy from school.

It had blank eyes. Below them were slits. These were its real eyes; the ones it saw with. On the shelves, encyclopaedias held their knowledge. Everything was here, except Nana.

Her father was asleep in Nana's chair, his head on a green wing.

A day after the news came he'd told Sarah that her mother had gone AWOL. Sarah didn't understand. He was suddenly the one to tuck her mosquito net in around her bed at night and make her breakfast in the morning; the one to drop her off at school. And he did everything wrong. He left gaps in the net, gave her a tablespoon to eat her cornflakes with, forgot the penny for her poke of roast groundnuts at break.

She knew not to say anything. She lay awake listening for the wail of mosquitos, swallowed her Rice Krispies from a tablespoon, accepted a small handful of nuts from Joseph Adeola and worried about what he'd want in return.

'Are you allowed to sit in that chair?' she asked now.

He stirred. 'Uh?'

'That's Nana's chair.'

Her father mumbled something.

Sarah stood in front of him. 'Tell me where my Nana is,' she said. It came out loud. 'Or don't you even know?'

Her father rose, his hand raised. Her own hands went up to cover her head. But his arm stopped in midair, as if someone had caught him by the wrist.

She sat down bump on a dining chair.

'Your grandmother's gone,' said her father. 'You won't be seeing her again. That's all you need to know, alright?'

On the mantelpiece, the golden balls of the carriage clock revolved oilily. The fire rustled like crinkly paper.

Her father sat back and said, 'Christ.' Then he said, 'Though when I say you won't be seeing her again, you will. In a way. She's coming back to the house tomorrow, so that your mother can say goodbye. So that the neighbours can pay their last respects. Then we can have the funeral.'

Sarah took the news in. 'I've never been to a human funeral,' she said. 'Will it be at night?'

Her father stared. 'You what? At this rate, we might decide you're too young to come to this one.'

'I'm not too young,' said Sarah.

Her father raised his hand again, but not in a bad way. 'Alright, alright. Let's not talk about it now. Let's get tomorrow over with first.'

He sighed. 'You see, when she comes tomorrow, it won't really be her. I mean, it will but it won't. You do understand, don't you?'

Sarah nodded. But it was obvious he was the one who didn't understand.

'Is she having a procession?' Perhaps he at least knew that.

'You what?' said her father.

She sighed. In Africa, even monkeys had processions.

The servants' monkey had lived on the end of a long chain. It was hardly ever let off because it made a beeline for the house and got in through a gap in the kitchen window. It loved to smash china and pull things to pieces, its whimper building to a scream, as if someone was being murdered.

When it died, it was laid quickly in a Dunlop shoebox before more insects came. Michael the cook tied its chin and its toes up with cloth.

'We tie mouth so monkey na speak,' he said. 'We tie toe so him na walk.'

Sarah stared at the tears that varnished his cheeks and dripped off his chin. She had never seen a man cry. From his shorts pocket Chidike brought the monkey's toy, a bent teaspoon it had spent hours turning over in its hands, perched on the handle of the garden fork that was its vantage point. He put the spoon in the box. Then he gave Sarah a bunch of twigs and told her to put them on top of the body. Looking at the monkey's pink curled hands, still raised to fight the spider that had bitten it, Sarah was sorry she had been afraid of it.

'Sesame tree, him grow hundred, hundred seed,' said Michael. 'Willi-willi come, him look for monkey spirit. But him na find. Him find only seed. Seed make problem for barawo devil, make plenty work. Him sit all night for to count. Monkey spirit is save for Papa God.'

Sarah nodded and didn't dare speak. The lid went on.

The procession had to be done in the dark to stop anyone's spirit following the monkey to the next realm. Back at the house, Sarah saw her mother passing to and fro behind the lit window in her orange dress, like a film star.

Before the first handfuls of dirt could rain down on the Dunlop box, Michael had to take Sarah's hand and lead her all over the compound behind Chidike, who carried it. They walked round and round and up and down, twisting and turning. It was to confuse the devil and stop the monkey spirit finding its way back. It was important to do everything right or the spirit might be restless and they would have to do the funeral all over again. Sarah fell into a trance watching Chidike's heels rise and fall in front of her, pale in the moonlight. She felt like a cog in a big smooth-running machine, and could have walked behind him forever.

Her father had fallen silent. She got up to put more coal on the fire, transferring shiny, uneven pieces from the bucket, using the blackened tongs. The coal made a thick blanket; the fire went out and the room cooled and grew darker. Sarah waited for a telling off, but her father's head had dropped onto his chest.

Sarah went round the house. She began with the front bedroom, where her mother was sleeping in the wide bed. Light from the streetlamp soaked the thin curtains and stained the whole room yellow. Sarah stood and listened to her mother breathe, soft as a distant sea.

She went back down the corridor to Nana's room, at the back of the house. The wardrobe loomed in the corner, like a night watchman. Sarah went to the single bed and ran her hand over the quilt, feeling its shine. She touched the bristles of Nana's hairbrush on the dressing table then opened her tub of face powder, sniffed the contents and coughed. She went to the window and peered down into the back garden; at the dark bulk of the shed. She wondered if the washing line and the apple tree were still there. Beyond the garden other houses had lit squares. There, normal things were probably happening, *like Top of the Pops* and *Dixon of Dock Green.*

No-one ever went in the front room. It housed the piano, three hard armchairs and a thick white rug with a design of pink and blue dragons. The rug came from China, and Nana forbade anyone to walk on it in their outdoor shoes.

Last was the kitchen. Tink, tink, went the water from the long rubber snout of the cold tap. Sarah switched the light on.

The brightness made everything shrink so she switched it off again. She crossed to the pantry, avoiding the black squares on the lino.

The pantry was indoors but felt like outdoors because the floor and shelves were made of stone slabs. Inside, Sarah touched Nana's tea caddy, black and shiny with red and gold Chinese figures. She reached inside a brown paper bag and touched tomatoes, cool and smooth. She peeped under waxed paper at sliced ham, shiny and white rimmed. In the metal bread bin was half a loaf that smelt funny and in the cake tin, half a cake that smelt of caraway seed, Nana's favourite.

The seeds were on the top shelf, in a jam jar. Sarah picked up all the jars in turn. Nutmegs nudged each other. Silver balls rattled. Glacé cherries sat tight, glued together with syrup. Sarah thought of all Nana's recipes: rice pudding, Easter biscuits, queen cakes, trifle. She saw Nana serving up tinned peaches and condensed milk as if it was a treat; saw her mother put her finger to her lips to stop Sarah saying it wasn't.

In the quiet, chilly pantry, she stayed still and concentrated hard, in case any luck was waiting to happen.

'Are you there, Nana?' she whispered.

She wasn't really expecting a reply. Nana never said much about herself, always wanted to hear your news first.

The next morning, when the men came, they trod all over the pink and blue dragons.

'Forget the damn rug,' said her mother, starting to cry. 'The important thing is that Mum's home.'

People arrived. The neighbour, Mrs Rampstead, came round three times and after every visit a crystal sherry glass stood upside down on the draining board. Mrs Rampstead eyed the mask on the mantelpiece and muttered about graven images and black magic. But Nana, who read the tealeaves, had loved magic. She'd once taken Sarah all round Gloucester to buy a wand. When they could only find a toy one, she said she didn't know what the covered market was coming to.

But Nana wasn't there to put Mrs Rampstead right. Sarah went upstairs and lay down on the floor in the narrow room behind the bathroom that used to be her uncle's.

You could hear people going to the toilet. You could hear the front door open and close, open and close; hear muffled sobs and moments later, laughter. Sarah thought people should be happy or sad, not both. Nana had a fault after all: she knew too many people.

No-one came up to see her, except her father, to bring her a sandwich of rubber cheese. When he'd gone, Sarah threw it out of the window. It got dark. When a rind of light appeared under the door, she got up.

In the back room, Sarah's mother sat in Nana's chair, gazing into the fire. Hope leapt in Sarah that she would smile or speak. But she didn't.

'I want to see Nana,' said Sarah.

Her father took cutlery out of a drawer. 'Not a good idea.'

The room stank of fish.. Three plump newspaper parcels lay by the fire. 'Please.'

Her father held up something silver. 'Are these what you mean by fish knives, Maureen?'

Her mother nodded. She looked at Sarah, but Sarah was scared by the swollen, blotchy face and looked away.

'I really want to see her,' she told her father. 'It's important.'

Her father shut the drawer. 'Well you can't. And there's an end to it.'

Sarah hoped her mother might look over again.

'You can see your grandmother in the morning,' her father said. 'Before they put the, err, lid on.'

'It'll be too late by then,' said Sarah.

'You what?' said her father, losing control of a newspaper parcel so that the fish flopped out onto the table.

Sarah glanced at her mother. But her mother's gaze had returned to the fire. There was something in there that she couldn't take her eyes off.

They went to bed. Sarah waited in her uncle's room, listening to the tick of the electric fire in the bathroom, the creak of the floorboards and the sighing of the airing cupboard, where Nana kept her ragbag and button box. The sounds eventually stopped, and she edged her way downstairs again, hanging off the banister to stop the stairs squeaking.

The front room was very dark. The coffin stood on trestles in the middle of the Chinese rug. The black and white china dogs looked down on its contents from the mantelpiece, but all Sarah could see was an edge of shiny white.

She needed something to stand on. She dragged the piano stool across to the coffin and climbed up, feeling the rough brocade under her bare knees.

Nana's hands, chilly and soft, had always been busy, stabbing a long pin into the hat that looked like a blackcurrant; conjuring the six o'clock news from the wireless; pecking crumbs from the chenille tablecloth. Or twisting the pages of the *Gloucester Citizen* into sticks for the fire; pressing warm half-crowns into Sarah's hand.

But now they were still, and Nana, her face secretive and waxy, held them crossed, useless on her chest. Sarah sank back onto her knees. Her father had been right, for once in his life. This both was and wasn't Nana.

In the kitchen, it was light as day. The moon beamed down onto the sink, the yellow Formica table and the kettle whose whistle was now at peace.

The stone flags in the pantry were so cold they hurt. Sarah smelt the ham again; saw the little men in golden robes drinking tea under the tree.

The moon shone through the high window onto the row of jam jars.

The jar she wanted stood between the angelica and the cloves.

She crept back through the kitchen, through the back room and into the hall where she stood, listening. Everything was still.

In the front room the dogs still gazed down, the piano still standing with its back to the wall baring its keys, and the coffin still pointed through the open curtains. But the room was filled with shadows, wedges and columns of dark that stretched out from the foot of things.

Sarah swallowed. But the piano stool stood firm as she climbed on. She looked down. Nana's skin was whiter, her nostrils darker and bigger, her eyes more deeply sunk in their sockets. She was getting deader by the minute.

Sarah was glad she knew what to do. She unscrewed the lid of the jam jar. The contents ran into her hand.

'I love you, Nana,' she whispered as she scattered the seed and watched it race over the dead face and hands and gather, darkly, in all the crevices and folds.

When My Doorbell Goes

When my doorbell goes these days, nine times out of ten it's the Jehovahs. Or jailbirds selling stupid products at stupid prices. No-one else calls. I flatten mesen against a wall; stay quiet as a mouse till they go. But the door's got frosted glass and today I gets caught.

It's a darkie.

I shout through the letter box. 'What do you want?'

He shows his teeth and holds a card against the glass. There's a photo but I can't see it.

'Is it the police?' I ask.

No answer. I open the door a crack.

His legs are right skinny in his shorts and he's carrying a blue Adidas bag. Cold air sweeps into the house. I wish I'd never opened the door. I step back, go to shut it.

The door bounces back. His foot, in a pink flip-flop, is over me threshold. Christ on a bike. Who wears flip-flops in February?

He says something.

'Speak English can't you?' I say.

'I am speaking in English, madame,' he says.

'Well it doesn't sound like it,' I say. 'What the bloody hell do you want?'

Then I realise his eyes are everywhere. Me door opens onto me sitting room and it's full of all bits and bobs. Plus the chairs look like they're covered in fur and the carpet's seen better days. I can't go up and down with the Hoover every verse end, not at my age, not with my foot.

'Madame, I can clean your house,' he says.

Of course I've been meaning to have a bit of a tidy. But the cat's gone diabetic. She's on special food, which I've to shop for. I have to get her to the vet every three months and that's no joke, not with the buses the way they are these days.

I open the door wider and he smiles. Probably thinks I'm about to ask him in. But I slam the door hard as I can onto his foot. It bounces back. He pulls his foot out sharpish. His eyes pop and saliva loops from his mouth. Disgusting.

'There's a lot going on at the moment,' I tell him. 'I've a lot on me mind. A cleaner is the last thing I want. Now bugger off and leave me alone.'

I shut the door.

Through the glass I see him crouched on the step clutching his foot. But what did he expect? Someone's got to show these folks.

That night I leave the pan on the heat and my baked beans turn to black lumps. I try and clean them off with wire wool but they're welded fast so the whole lot goes in't wheelie bin. Waste of a good pan. The black lad has that on his conscience too.

Saturday morning, me neighbour comes round. Sarah, she's called. She's younger 'an me but she's on her own, too. Sits on the sofa between the bin bags, tells me about her week at the hozzie; folks arriving too early, too late, not having drunk enough water and one silly cow who went into labour on the couch. They don't mind what they talk about these days. How she can stand looking at unborn babies all day when she never, you know, beats me. She says they've delayed retirement for her age group. I doubt that, but I don't say owt. She sips the coffee like it's poison.

'Is there sugar in this?' she says.

So skinny she is, scared of food. She's old enough to know better.

'That'll be the milk,' I say. 'I ran out of fresh, used condensed.'

She goes all strict on me. 'Have you been out this week?' she says.

I haven't the foggiest but I say, 'Yes, let's see, Tuesday I think it was. I walked to t'shops.'

'Did you put your teeth in?'

How'm I supposed to remember that? 'Expect so,' I say.

'And your hearing aid?'

She paid for that. I didn't ask her to. But guess who has to pay for t'batteries? Twenty pence each, rip off.

'I don't recollect,' I say.

She looks tired.

'Do you want a Crawford's wafer?' I ask.

They're me favourite but she shakes her head. Wrong sort of carbs apparently, whatever they are. Oats are the right sort. She likes ginger oatcakes but I won't give 'em house room.

The conversation peters out. I don't know why she comes.

Next day the druggie, or whatever, is back on the other side of t'glass panel.

I think about me ruined pan.

'You've got a brass neck,' I tell him.

I try think up an insult about his beard an' big teeth but

can't. Sometimes when I'm angry, the words come better than normal. Today they don't.

'I said no work and I meant no work,' I say.

'I am come to ask if you have second thoughts,' he says.

His foot is like a balloon but I'm blowed if I'm going to feel guilty. 'No I haven't,' I say. 'If I wanted a cleaner, I'd get a woman.'

She comes to mind, no-nonsense with short grey hair, equipped with her own rubber gloves and cleaning fluids.

'And I'd pick someone English,' I say. I don't like to say white. You don't want to sound racist.

'You prefer English woman house cleaner,' he says.

'Got it in one,' I say.

'You have advertised for this cleaner?'

That takes me aback. 'Well, no,' I say. 'Not that it's any of your business.'

He nods. 'I am hard worker, better than a feeble woman.'

He thrusts a card into me hand. An address, 49 Spencer Place. I know that street: everyone does. They sell sex on one corner, fried chicken on the other.

'All I ask is, give me free trial,' he says. 'I am very hard worker.'

He smiles with his big teeth. I could do with a few of those myself. I can suck oranges with me denture, but that's about it.

'Don't you understand English?' I say. 'I don't want a cleaner. I don't want a stranger poking their nose in.'

'Understand,' he says. 'But Madame is home now?'

'I'm standing here right in front of you, aren't I,' I cry.

'Madame is home for half hour?'

I stare at him. Hasn't he heard a word I've said?

'I do free trial now, clean house in thirty minute,' he says.

'You have products, yes? If work no good, Madame then does not hire me.'

'I don't want you cleaning now,' I shout. 'I'm going out in a minute.'

I look down at my slippers. 'I was about to put me shoes on,' I say.

'Tomorrow,' he says. 'Any time. Ten. Eleven. Twelve. I give the house once-over.'

'No,' I say. 'I've got things to do tomorrow. Urgent things!'

'Wednesday. I come Wednesday. I show you good work.'

I stare at him. What do folk do to get out of things these days? Go out and buy a gun, I suppose. But this isn't America. It's not even Manchester, or Gunchester as I've 'eard 'em call it these days. It's bloody Leeds.

'I'll get my son onto you,' I say.

My son's in Australia, or was last I heard. But the lad won't know that.

'Madame,' he says, 'I come then on Wednesday.'

I look at him. He's skinny as a lath but he's got a big frame. If he's going to rob and murder me, he'll do it anyway so why not get it over with, I think.

'Oh for God's sake,' I say, 'if you're that keen, come in and do it now.'

'Madame, I thank you,' he says. 'Madame is angel lady, gift from God. I give you free trial now. Show me Vim, show me bucket.'

If I wasn't so busy preparing mesen to be robbed and murdered, I'd have found that quite charming.

'You've done what?' My neighbour stops in the aisle of the

garden centre, between the lavender and lemon balm. She's brought me here to take me out of mesen.

'It's only until he gets a proper job,' I say.

You see, he didn't rob and murder me, did he. He donned pink Marigolds and cleaned my toilet. Then he washed all my skirting boards. Grey scum all over: I hadn't realised how mucky they'd got. He was limping.

'It was an accident,' I said. 'I didn't see your foot in't door.'

'A misunderstanding,' he said. I was surprised he knew such a long word.

I told him I'd a bad foot too from my deeveetee. He asked if he could make me a cuppa. Does he know how to work a kettle, I thought. I must have said it out loud because he laughed and said back in Aba he was a trained electrician. He said did I want a light putting in the under stairs cupboard. I told him I didn't like rushing into things. Then he said he'd work for three pounds an hour.

'But can he clean properly?' my neighbour asks.

'Not bad,' I say, 'and anyway at that price who cares? It's got to be an improvement.'

'Is three pounds an hour even legal?' she says.

'I didn't suggest it,' I say, 'he did.'

'How d'you know he is who he says he is?' she says.

'He's got papers.'

'What sort of papers? References?'

'Yes.' He give me a bit of paper with pencil on. From someone called the Chinaman. A kind man, he said, though he didn't say why. I couldn't read it. Glasses these days are useless. They give you double vision.

'But what's behind it,' says my neighbour.

'Nothing's behind it,' I say.

We go into a conservatory of tomato plants. They smell of vinegar. I like it here; you can walk for miles hanging on to the trolley. That's more than you can do at the day centre.

But my neighbour's gone strict again.

'Cynthia,' she says, 'it's twenty-sixteen.'

I sigh. They're always on at me about dates. Do I know what month it is, what year. Do I know who's prime minister. How can you, when there's a new one every ten minutes?

'The world's a dangerous place these days,' she says.

It always was, dear, I think.

'You must be careful who you open your door to,' she says.

I touch a tomato flower, so delicate you'd never think it could turn into a big red fruit. They've got runner beans in here too. Pretty leaves but if you put them outside this early, they'll die. Not that the folks at the garden centre care.

'Are you listening to me?' she asks. 'If you want a cleaner why don't you go to a proper agency, make sure it's all above board?'

'I should have thought that was obvious,' I say.

She looks blank. Medically trained maybe, but she's no common sense.

'Because anyone with the word agent in their job title gets paid a small fortune for doing beggar all,' I say. 'Look at estate agents: all crooks.'

She ignores me; starts on about safety. When she sees me face she says, 'Anyway what's the problem, you can afford it.'

How does she know, I think and keep schtum as we head for the cafe through the room of aprons, coasters and shortbread.

'At least let me meet him,' she says.

I wish she'd find herself a decent husband. Then she'd stop poking her nose into my affairs.

'That's harsh,' she says, 'when I'm only trying to look out for you.'

Oh dear, I must've said it aloud. I try and smooth things. 'It's just, I doubt you'd get time off work,' I say.

'Can't he come when I'm off?'

In the cafe, she stops at the coffee machine, presses the button. All that milk! She tops it with cocoa powder. They kid themselves they're not eating but they drink half a pint of milk and call it coffee.

'Anyway, he's got another job,' I say. 'He's going to fit me in when he can.'

'Another job doing what?'

'Putting supplements into Sunday newspapers.'

'Where? And where's he from in the first place?'

But I'm fed up of being cross-examined. I want to sit with my cuppa looking out the window at the daffs. Or listen to one of her stories again, like about the woman who was given 36G breasts for her thirtieth birthday.

'I'll get him to come when you're off,' I say. 'You can ask all your questions then.'

She presses a button and hot water pours down into my little metal kettle. Machines, machines. Where did real people go?

As it happens, the next two times he comes, she's at work. But he gets the sitting room done. He tells me the carpet were all stained. I doubt that. It's a good carpet, nice pattern, better than today's rubbish. He puts vinegar on the windows. They're so clean, I have to touch them to check the glass is still in. It's like there's more air in the room now the bin bags are in t'cupboard. Turns out the cupboard was empty but how was I to know; I could never get to it to find out.

The third time, he turns up as usual but he looks iffy. Don't ask me how a darkie can look pale, but he does.

He leaves his Adidas bag by the door. I don't know why he bothers with it. It's empty: I sneaked a look.

He wants to talk about my oven. 'It is gas, Mrs Hammond?'

I've put him right on that Madame business. It got on my shetlap.

'Gas hob,' I say. 'The rest is 'lectric.'

'When this oven clean last time, Mrs Hammond?'

The burner I use most is all bobbled with a ring round it like a brown doily.

'I've been busy,' I say. 'The cat has to have her injections. And I have to weigh all her food.'

'Understand,' he says. 'But viewing panel is dirty. Health and safety is not correct. I remove glass, I soak in soda. Grease come free while I am in bedroom, wash window, Hoover under bed.'

It's all a bit much to take in.

'You do not want this hazard in kitchen,' he says.

I try to think. I'm not sure about the glass coming out. And I hadn't reckoned on the bedroom. What if he looks under the floorboards?

'Who is not getting your savings?' he asks. I must've said me thoughts out loud again. I don't know when I'm doing it, that's the trouble. I feel awkward.

'Nothing,' I say. 'Go ahead.'

'Good,' he says. 'You must not sleep in this dust.'

He makes my usual cuppa then goes up, starts making clonking noises.

I sit at the table with my *Daily Mail,* reading the same bit over and over. It goes quiet upstairs. I picture him sitting on the bed counting my money. Or he could've robbed the lot already, be shinning down the drain pipe and away.

I can't settle.

I make a racket going up. My foot's bad and I catch my stick on the skirting board. But then you should always let burglars know you're coming.

The bedroom door is open so I walk in.

My mouth falls open. He's not sitting on the bed, counting money; he's laying there with his head on me pillow. I stand there like an idiot then I shuffle across, grab the padded head-board and lift my stick to prod him. But he turns onto his front and his hand flops against my leg. It stops me dead. He curls his hand round my knee. My breath sticks in my throat. I should scream but instead all I can think is that no-one touches me these days except the dentist and the doctor and that's not the sort of touch you want. The black lad's touch int meant for me, I know that much, so I'm down the stairs and out the front door. I'm banging on next door's with me stick. I'm practically in tears.

Of course she's never there when you need her. I go on hammering. I mean who works on a ruddy Saturday? But the concrete's cold under me slippers and I don't want to exacerbate me foot. I'll have to face him on me own the way I've faced every other situation for the past forty years. I go back.

'Son,' I call up the stairs. He told me his name, but it were something unpronounceable I hoped I'd never have to say. 'Son, it's time to wake up.'

No reply so I go upstairs. Up and down like a bloody yo-yo it is today.

He's not there. He must've gone out the back. No dint in the counterpane, even. Destroyed the evidence. I hobble to my floorboard, expecting my life savings gone. But me rolls of twenties are all still there, tight and oily. Downstairs the coins I put on the table for him are still there too. I start putting them back in my purse but can't. They stay by the fruit bowl, gold and silver.

Later I change the pillowcase but seeing as how he never got in the bed, I leave the sheets. I decide not to tell her next door. She'd only say she told me so.

But when she brings my shopping the next morning and we sit down to a brew, I end up telling her most of it, though I scale the money down to four hundred not four thousand and don't let on how he held me knee and made me nearly blub. She might think I want a hug.

'He must've been exhausted,' she says.

'Hardly the point,' I say. 'Bloody Nigerian.'

Her eyes go wide. 'You never said he was from Nigeria. Where in Nigeria?'

'How do I know,' I say. 'Abracadabra? Something like that.'

'Aba? Was it Aba?'

'Might have been,' I say.

'I went to school in Aba,' she said. 'We lived there for two years.'

'You?' I say. 'Now I've heard everything.'

'So is he fleeing from Boko Haram,' she says, 'did he say?'

'Boko who?' I say. 'All I know is, I paid him to do a job and he never did it.'

'Yes but you didn't, did you,' she says. 'He didn't take the money.'

'True,' I say and we sit there looking at each other.

The weeks go by. Apple blossom drops from the trees. I go to the under-stairs cupboard, flicks me new switch. It lights up the Hoover, the see-through drum full of grey muck. Dead skin cells, they say. I feel queasy.

Next thing, I have an up and downer with the newsagents.

When next door comes round, I'm agitated. She's brought me a tray of violas and I snatch them off her. We go down to the kitchen.

'What's the matter?' she says.

'Nothing,' I say. The violas hit the draining board so hard their purple and yellow faces quiver.

'Oh, alright,' I say. 'That bloody newsagent is buggering me about.'

'Have you paid his bill recently?' she asks.

She holds the kettle to the tap. The water rises inside it like music but I'm too upset to enjoy it. 'Of course I have,' I say.

'When?' she asks. 'When did you last pay it?'

'I don't know,' I say. 'Anyway, he's just a kid. A bloody kid talking to me 'bout direct debits. "Direct debits?" I said, "How old are you? I'm reporting you to *Watchdog*. I'm going to get myself a gun and shoot the bloody lot of you."'

She sighs.

'That boy who came to do your cleaning,' she asks. 'I think he did you good.'

I've no idea what she's talking about.

The kettle rattles, she fishes cups and saucers from the

drainer and we go up to the sitting room. Now t'windows are clean, I've had to resurrect t'net curtains to shut out prying eyes. Turns out dirt had a use after all.

'Did you ever get his address?' she asks.

'Whose address,' I say, though I know fine well.

She pours the tea.

'I threw it away, why? It was Spencer Place,' I say, 'that I do remember.'

'What number,' she asks.

'I forget,' I say. 'It was an odd number.'

Next time we have a brew it's at the garden centre. I'm sat next to a giant yucca that costs £650.

She tells me about a woman who brought a plastic bag of potatoes into the Ultrasound room. They perched, all earthy, on top of her wire basket of clothes while she had her scan. We laugh about that one.

Then she says, 'I went to Spencer Place.'

The end of me Rich Tea Finger drops off into me tea.

I try and remember when I were last down Spencer Place and I can't. It must have been a bloody long time ago. As a child you got warned not to go down there. As a young woman it were out of bounds too, in case a kerb crawler thought you were fair game.

'Weren't you frightened?' I ask.

She laughs. 'Frightened,' she asks, 'what of? Another radiologist lives there.'

'Does he indeed,' I say, not believing it for a moment, doctors and such living in a place like that.

'"She",' she says, 'not "he". It's a lovely big house. She's doing it up.'

I fish soggy biscuit out on the end of my teaspoon and say nowt.

'Anyway,' she says, 'I looked at all the odd numbers. You could rule most of them out; rainbow decals in the window, onion crops in the front garden. But there were a couple of possibles; concreted front gardens, lots of wheelie bins out the front, you know the sort of thing.'

'I don't,' I say. 'You know fine well our neighbourhood's owner-occupier and I've not been out of it in years.'

She sighs. 'Alright,' she says, 'anyway a boy on a BMX came over, asked who I was looking for. I had to give him a fiver but he told me which house. He balanced on his pedals the whole time we were talking, never put his foot down once.'

'A fiver?' I say. 'That's a bit steep.'

'Boat people,' she says, 'that's what he called them.'

She frowns into her coffee. 'Oh Cynthia, only one window had any glass, in the dormer. The others were all boarded up. And there was, well, excrement smeared on the front door. I'd written a card for him. It was a cartoon dog. Silly! I pushed it through the door anyway. I told him to get in touch. Told him we'd pay more.'

'Do you think I'm made of money,' I say.

'God,' she says. 'I'll pay.'

'Are you a charity now,' I say. She doesn't reply.

I swallow a bit of biscuit. I'm thinking about the black lad. All things being equal, I hope he's not in trouble.

'I hope he lives in that dormer with the glass,' I blurt, 'among all the chimneys and treetops.'

She stares at me. She reaches across the table and squeezes my hand. It's becoming regular now, folk touching me for no reason.

We're nearly into summer. All the plants and trees are out, a right show. I prefer February, when there's just snowdrops and crocus, there for them as knows how to look.

The newsagent gets me going again. I've gone in with a few twenties off one of me rolls. Olive branch, so to speak. Instead of looking grateful he says that these are old ones, they've got Edward Elgar on.

'Edward who,' I ask.

'They stopped being legal tender in twenty-ten,' he says.

'What?' I ask.

'I can't accept them,' he says. 'You'll have to apply to the Bank of England. They'll redeem them.'

'You should spend more time doing your job,' I say, 'instead of standing smoking out the back. I've seen you.'

But it rings a bell. It were on the news.

'The Bank of England's in bloody London,' I say. 'You expect me to go all the way down there on the coach, with my foot?'

That gives him a jolt. 'Oh well, I don't know, he says. Isn't there a branch in Leeds?'

Then something strikes me and I go and blurt it out. 'I've got four thousand pound in Edward Elgar money under me blimmin' floorboards,' I say. 'It's what I've scrimped and saved all me life for. Are you telling me it's worthless?'

His eyes dart about the shop and he's saying, 'Keep your voice down, Mrs Hammond,' and getting me a chair and a glass of water from out the back.

The woman comes out. She's a kid too. She calls me Cynthia and her just out of school! Don't you worry, she tells me, 'We'll sort your bill out for you. We'll change these notes ourselves.' She pats my hand like they all do these days.

'I bet you will,' I say. I stand up and the water goes all over. 'Well, I know who's got my address. When the money goes missing I'll know who's tekken it.'

She's all 'Oh no, that's not what I meant', but I'm out of there and along that pavement as fast as my foot can carry me.

Back home the key sticks in the lock.

I hear a voice behind me.

'What is matter? Mrs Hammond. Are you sick?'

'Christ,' I say, 'not you an' all. I've been worried half to death about you but why do you have to turn up now? I'm in the midst of a crisis. I've got things on my mind.'

He's still in his shorts and flip-flops. Don't they change their clothes in Nigeria?

'I can help,' he says.

'I'm capable of opening my own bloody door!' I shout.

Then suddenly I'm sitting on the path, my keys in the flower bed. Did he push me?

'Oh take the lot!' I shout. 'Take it and do what you like. Throw a party for all your friends, I don't care; I'll be gone soon. Then you can dance on my grave.'

'What is this you are talking,' he says, and pulls me to my feet.

Inside, he leaves his Adidas by the door, sets me on the sofa, goes down to the kitchen. When he comes back, I'm blubbing my eyes out. I don't know what it is, the fall, the shock, or what.

He takes my hand, passes me a cup.

'Drink,' he says. 'You will feel better.'

I sip it. It's tea but it's sickly, warming. Maybe he's put a shot of cooking sherry in.

He's brought up a bowl of water and a cloth.

'You're not cleaning now, are you?' I say. My breath comes in shudders.

No, he tells me, and kneels down. He opens the Velcro on my shoe and takes my foot out. He dabs it through me stocking. It stings like beggary but I let him carry on. I can't bend down to do it myself.

That's when I notice he looks different, teeth missing. 'What's happened to you?' I say.

He touches the top lip where the teeth once were.

'Fight arrive with white man,' he says, 'no reason.'

There's always a reason. But I don't like to say so, not with his poor teeth gone.

'Did you get our card?' I remember. He looks blank. 'She pushed it through your door: me neighbour. Spencer Place.'

He shakes his head. 'Spencer Place finish long time.'

Under the dirt me foot's red. You can see it through the American Tan. He starts on me knee. My tights are torn, I must've banged it.

'So where have you been living,' I ask.

He dips the cloth in the rusty water. 'Am sleep in cupboard from Chinaman,' he says. 'Chinaman good friend. But cupboard finish also.'

Living in a cupboard, I tell him. I've never heard anything like it. He shrugs. 'How long for,' I say.

'Many week,' he says, dabbing, dabbing. 'But now shift is change. Finish three, start again five. Cupboard is now taken, next sleeper is there. Shift finish in day, am sleep in park maybe. Shift finish in night, is too cold. In Wakefield, see African mens walk on pavement, walk, walk.'

I stare at him. I know Wakefield's going down but darkies

walking the streets all night, getting into fights? I don't know what to make of it.

I realise the door's still open. It's a decent neighbourhood but you've got to be careful. I get the feeling there's more of them on the doorstep, waiting to come in. I try and see them better but the blue Adidas gets in my line of vision.

'Show yourselves!' I shout.

'What are you talking now,' says the lad. I push his hand away. 'Not finish, Mrs Hammond,' he says. 'Let me finish, please. Is important I get all this dirt out.'

'But what about the men,' I say.

'What mens?' He gets up and goes to the door. 'No mens outside,' he says.

But he doesn't shut the door. And I know they're there. 'Come in and make yourselves known!' I shout.

He shakes his head. As though I'm some sort of halfwit.

He starts on me knee again.

I wish the men would come in, or go away. But they go on standing there, waiting to make their move. I can almost see them, blurred behind the frosted glass.

Current Affairs

The teacher stood under the fan. The rainy season was late, the classroom hot as a kiln. A mesh window divided the outside world into parched squares.

'I am setting up a discussion group,' he told the class. Sweat tickled the inside of his arms. 'The first meeting is at four o'clock today.'

Twelve boys sat still under the low ceiling.

'The atmosphere will be informal,' the teacher had said in an encouraging tone. 'It will give you a chance to express your opinions. It will be most enjoyable!'

He smiled, thinking of his old English master, a column of charcoal grey who addressed the clock at the back of the room, on and on, even when he was talking only to you. He didn't want to be that teacher.

But the silence deepened. Boys made detailed studies of the cement floor.

The teacher frowned. They were thinking, perhaps, that four o'clock was their rest period, when they sat in their dormitories like fishermen with needle and thread mending their mosquito nets. Or ran down the track to the river to wash their shirts and shorts and shove each others' heads under the water.

But there was no other time the group could be held. He'd had to fight to hold it at all.

'No, no, no,' the head had said, orange in his brocade tunic and hat, bejewelled sandals. He'd strode about while the teacher sat timid on a straight-backed chair. 'Your idea is not a good idea. The boys are here to pass their exams. They are here to gain their places at university. They are not here to indulge in idle chit-chat.'

The teacher had cited the British school system. Debate, he'd said. Persuasive discourse. Talking around a subject. Grounding in current affairs, he'd added, when the head glanced at his watch. History in the making. Take this morning's news. I picked it up in French, on Congolese radio. President Kennedy has sent a fleet to Cuba.

When the head asked how the learnings from the new group would be tested, the teacher, knowing he'd won, wanted to punch the air. Instead, he forced himself to talk about scored group discussion.

He hadn't realised he would have to sell the group to the boys too.

'We can talk about all sorts of things,' he said to them now. 'Enjoyable subjects. Matters of, um, personal interest. I don't mean the facts of life,' he added quickly, his face hot. 'And I realise that four o'clock is normally your free time. But it won't hurt to give it up once a week.'

One boy, Gideon, who was given to frowning, often spoke on behalf of the others. In fact he was the only boy who spoke at all.

'Sa,' he said now, not putting his hand up first. He had what the teacher thought of as a regal bearing. 'The time of the class is not important to us.'

'Oh,' said the teacher.

'Neither do we wish to enjoy the lessons,' said Gideon. The teacher's eyes widened. 'Is only,' said Gideon, 'we do not understand what are these opinions, what are these informal atmospheres.'

'Well, they're *your* opinions,' said the teacher. 'They're what you think; what you believe. And an informal atmosphere... well, it's a session where the format is less structured, more relaxed.'

Two boys wrote in their exercise books. The teacher was satisfied with his definitions.

But the furrows on Gideon's forehead deepened. 'Sa, I do not have opinions. Even if I did, they would certainly be worthless.'

'Worthless,' echoed the teacher.

'Who is it that you see in this room,' asked Gideon, looking round at the rest of the class. His tone had an edge of impatience.

Gideon will make a good politician, thought the teacher. His father was a village chief. 'Go on,' he said.

'I will tell you,' said Gideon. 'You see boys.'

'Of course,' said the teacher.

'What I mean is that you do not see men,' said Gideon.

'Oh,' said the teacher. 'Well, most of you are fourteen. You're well on the way.'

Several of the boys were more like sixteen, going by their height and incipient beards. Not that it mattered. He was being sidetracked as usual. He tried to treat everyone the same but just as the radio in his room was permanently tuned to the Congolese station, so in the classroom his senses were permanently tuned to Gideon.

Gideon let out a long sigh, as if he was the teacher. He said that being on the way was not the same as having arrived at the final destination.

'Perhaps I'm not explaining myself as well as I might,' said the teacher, remembering too late that it was a bad idea to admit failure.

He was saved by the classroom door opening. A man in a red turban entered and ushered in five other men in business suits, who assembled near the blackboard. He nodded to the teacher, then turned to his guests and told them that this was a typical learning environment of the region. 'Here we witness a teacher equipping the children of our province with the skills our country needs at this time of great change, at this time of great progress.'

The men gazed about the room listlessly then stood as if the waiting for the future to happen before their very eyes.

The interruption had given the teacher time to collect himself. He said they would now begin the lesson proper. As for the discussion group, attendance was voluntary and if anyone wished to find out more, he had merely to turn up at four o'clock. Boys from other classes and subject groups would be present and it would be a good opportunity to work alongside them.

Between three and four, the teacher was free to walk down to the river. Dark vegetation he couldn't yet name towered on either side of him. The track was hard underfoot but apparently in the rainy season it plastered your legs with mud.

The river, low and sluggish at the moment, was known as a miracle river. A local herdsman had witnessed it spring up in a field and become five feet deep within seconds. A local octogenarian said it appeared every twenty years to prevent evil. A mile away it formed an ox bow, where food vendors did good business catering to the hordes that came from all over the province to bathe in the waters or drink them.

The teacher was scared of snail fever, a waterborne disease, so even though dabbling his fingers in the waters might have healed him, he contented himself by watching the sky's reflection move slowly downstream. He would talk about key inventors of Britain he decided; show the boys how individuals could shape history.

Back in London, he'd read everything he could about the country's challenges now that independence had been declared. What happened in these early years could define the future. That was why he had wanted to come, even to this school in the middle of nowhere with paraffin lamps and no running water. And he was glad to be here. Even though the real Africa was different to the way it was in the *Boy's Own* adventures he'd read as a child.

He went back to the classroom and wrote *18th century Britain: the Industrial Revolution* on the blackboard.

Ten minutes later, eight boys filed into the classroom. The teacher was pleased and alarmed to see Gideon among them, immaculate in his white shirt, even at the end of the school day.

The teacher started with Richard Arkwright's invention for the cotton spinning wheel then moved on to James Watt's improvements to the steam engine. He'd told the boys not to make notes, but they bent over their exercise books and he talked more than he meant to, drawn by the very notetaking he wanted to discourage. At last he stopped.

'Put your pens down,' he said.

The boys looked up, surprised. Only one or two put down their pens.

'You don't need to write down everything I say verbatim,' said the teacher. 'It's too passive.' Two boys wrote that down. 'I would prefer you to talk,' said the teacher.

'But how will we be tested on mere talking, sa,' asked Gideon.

'I will award marks as we go along,' said the teacher. 'Later. Don't worry about it now. For the time being let's just get the discussion going. I won't be able to test you at all, if you never talk!'

The boys looked anxious.

'So,' said the teacher, 'does anyone know why I am telling you about things that happened two hundred years ago in a country very different to yours?'

No-one spoke. Gideon put his hand up. The teacher nodded at him, hopeful. 'We do not know, sa,' said Gideon.

The teacher had to provide his own answer. He spoke about drawing on the lessons that history teaches us. 'Only a fool,' he said, 'learns from his own mistakes. The wise man learns from the mistakes of others.'

'Sa,' said Gideon, 'this is a fine saying. Is it your invention?'

The teacher was tempted to say it was. But it wasn't worth it. One of the boys would find him out. 'No,' he said.

'Who then is the author?' asked Gideon.

The teacher couldn't remember. But he didn't want to detract from the moment. William Shakespeare, he told them with confidence, although he knew it was not William Shakespeare. The boys wrote it down.

The teacher had prepared a list of questions about the country's economy. He wrote them on the blackboard. His arm ached; the chalk made his fingers dry and white. But the boys looked blank – he had not found the subject that would make them talk. Again, he had to supply his own answers. Canoe fisheries, he wrote. Cocoa; ground nut; guinea corn. The Niger Agricultural Project.

Changing the topic seemed too much like backing down and

anyway he had nothing else prepared. He talked for ten minutes about possible ways to mechanise the production of palm oil, a subject he knew very little about, and they wrote it all down.

The following week, he decided to try something different. He had just finished reading a novel by Chinua Achebe and he brought his copy of the book to class.

The same eight boys as before were there. The school uniform included brown sandals but by four o'clock, most of them had come off. He decided not to mention it.

The English syllabus, he informed them, focused mainly on white writers from the previous century. 'I would like to introduce you to a celebrated author from your own culture. A contemporary voice.'

He began reading aloud from the novel. So moved was he to remember the fate of the central character, Okonkwo, a fate he had learnt a few nights ago in the guttering light of his kerosene lamp, that he read for ten minutes without stopping.

When he looked up, he saw bored faces.

He felt disappointed. 'This is just the start of the story,' he said, his voice trembling slightly. 'Mr Achebe goes on to write about the effects of colonialism in your country.'

You could tell when the boys were displeased. They sank their heads between their shoulders or rolled them round on their necks. The reasons for their displeasure were not so obvious, though. The teacher was still recovering from their scowls at his use of red ink to mark their exercise books. He was still puzzling over their unhappiness at being asked to use their imaginations.

'You must bear with the narrative a little longer,' he

said sternly. 'I shall read on.'

Gideon interrupted. 'Why must we hear about this ignorant man?' he asked. 'A man who values fighting above all other things?'

The teacher was startled. Mr Achebe's novel was widely respected in the West, he told them. 'It's regarded as a modern classic, one of the most important works of world literature in recent years.'

'A man who despises even his own father,' said Gideon. The book's central character was Igbo. The teacher worried suddenly about this. The school was a boarding school, and the boys came from all over the region. Some were Igbo, he supposed. Perhaps it was a sensitive matter? He didn't know; should have checked with one of the other teachers. He began to sweat. 'How can a writing about a lowly bush man be valued all over the world,' Gideon went on.

The teacher was too uncertain to defend the book. He decided to cut his losses. Never mind for now, he told them. 'We will come back to Mr Achebe. Don't think you are getting off scot free, however. I'm determined that you will come to appreciate and even love this fine modern classic!' He tittered, to show he was being light hearted, but Gideon sighed heavily, as if disappointed.

The session turned into another lecture, this time about the importance of World Literature. Afterwards, the teacher realised that he had closed down the first real chance for debate. He asked another teacher, an American Peace Corps volunteer named Jerry, about the tribal issue. But the long-haired young man shrugged. 'Nope,' he said. 'Wish I could help you, man. But this tribal jizz is outside of my experience and then some.'

The following week when the group assembled, Gideon wasn't among them. Trying not to wonder why, the teacher wrote some questions on the blackboard in squeaking chalk. They were things he himself was curious about; had been since his arrival three weeks ago.

'What is your father's occupation?' he wrote. 'Do you come from an educated family or are you the first to receive schooling?' 'Are your sisters encouraged to attend school?' 'As a child, did your father spend time with you and if so, what did you do together?' He wrote down a few more similar questions then turned and offered the boys an encouraging smile. 'Would anyone like to begin the discussion by answering one of these questions?' he asked.

The boys focussed on various body parts.

Perhaps some personal things were easier to talk about than others. He wrote down a few more questions. By the time he'd reached the end of his list, he'd discovered they weren't.

He surprised himself by wishing that Gideon was there. Although he often wanted to throttle the boy, he decided now that what he'd seen as presumption was generosity; the boy offering himself as a bridge between teacher and class.

He felt very alone. 'Well boys,' he said, trying to sound jolly, 'you don't seem to be in a very talkative mood today. Perhaps it would help if I answered some of the questions first, from my own experience? Perhaps that would, ah, encourage you. My father is an archaeologist. So is my mother. Education has always been highly prized in my family. As for sisters... well, I don't have any. Or brothers, for that matter. I'm an only child.' Curious glances. 'I know that's unusual in your country. But in Britain it's common.' He wondered if this were true. At his own school and later at university, he had only ever met two other only children. 'Some couples decide not to have a family at all. And of course, some can't.'

A boy clicked his tongue.

The teacher pressed on. 'As for spending time with my father,' he said, 'I hardly did. Though he once took me to a football match. That's something fathers do with sons, in England. Especially working class-fathers. Not that my father was working class. Far from it.'

They had seen Tottenham Hotspur. He remembered nothing about the game. What he remembered was squeezing through the high clanking turnstile; the warmth of the greasy Cornish Pasty that his Dad said to keep schtum about when they got home. He remembered the great male roar when a goal was scored, a force at his back.

He was lost for a moment in speculation about his father and why he had taken him there.

When he looked up, several boys had their hands up.

'Oh,' said the teacher, surprised. He nodded at a tall very dark-skinned boy called Moses.

'Do you know Bobby Charlton, sa?' the boy asked hopefully.

The teacher had never heard Moses speak before. 'I'm afraid not,' he said. A memory came, of a young man with dark Brylcreemed hair flourishing a felt-tipped pen. 'Though I did meet Alf Ramsey. He signed my football.'

'Do you still have this football, sa? Can you show it to me?' asked Moses.

'I do,' said the teacher. 'But I didn't bring it to Nigeria.'

Moses looked astonished, thinking perhaps that if he owned such a treasure, he would never allow himself to be parted from it.

'Sa, were you involved in the 1958 Munich Air Disaster?' asked another boy.

'Not personally, Elijah,' said the teacher.

But the accident had received so many column inches in the papers that he was able to remember how it had happened, the names of all the players who'd died. He told the class how manager Matt Busby was rebuilding Manchester United.

More hands shot up. He could hardly believe it was happening.

More boys whose voices he had never heard asked about Real Madrid; Inter Milan. They wanted to know what he thought about the Brazilian player Pele.

He knew nothing about international football. But the boys' interest was like a spell, enabling him to string convincing sentences together from the papers, past conversations, Congolese radio, even.

'Ferenc Puskas!' A boy shouted from the back, adding that in his opinion, Puskas was the greatest footballer who had ever lived because he was also the best team player who had ever lived. Now other boys joined in, putting forth the merits of their own favourites.

'One at a time, boys,' said the teacher. He tried to sound stern but his pink cheeks gave him away.

The monitor came down the corridor and rang his bell outside the classroom door. Had forty minutes really passed?

'Alright,' the teacher shouted above the clang. 'Enough is enough. I will see you all next week.' He turned to wipe the board with a damp cloth.

The boys continued talking into the corridor, animated. The teacher listened to their voices recede. Feeling swelled in his chest and he knew himself to be fully here at this time, in this country, in this classroom drenched in late-afternoon sunshine. A boy laughed somewhere and it was a gentle sound, hardly disturbing the quiet.

The Sea Spirit

Different parents are taking Johnny to the coast for the weekend. They've made him sit next to their daughter Sarah in the back of the Chevrolet. You're almost exactly the same age, they keep saying. As though that means anything.

The road to the coast is long and bumpy. His legs swim on the seat and through the open window, dust blows into his eyes. The servant, Chidike, is perched on the edge of the back seat between them, and every time the car swerves to avoid bullfrogs or whatever, he bangs his head on the ceiling. Johnny doesn't like servants, but his father said get used to it, son, because even people like us have servants out here.

The mother teaches English at the school, though she doesn't teach Johnny because he is in the bottom tier. Sarah is in the top tier. Her mother is tall and bony, nothing like Johnny's mother, who is soft and quiet. He doesn't know what to call the other mother: Miss or Aunty Maureen, so he avoids speaking to her at all. The mother turns round and frowns at the servant from time to time, which makes the servant laugh. He seems to think everything is funny. Johnny is pretty sure that some things aren't funny.

The holiday huts are made of bamboo and have pointy roofs. While the servant unloads the car, Johnny kicks at the sand. It's soft and white. Monkeys swing in a clump of trees a little way off. The mother tells them, you two run along for a paddle and a cool down. Sarah runs straight for the sea, but Johnny looks at the mass of water creeping up and down the beach and roaring softly and his legs go weak.

He has always been scared of water. His grandmother was dropped over the side of the Liverpool ferry when she was a baby. I was borne up on my swaddling clothes, she always says, her eyes beady and shining, but I've never set foot in a boat since. When Johnny says he'll never set foot in a boat either, she taps his hand and calls him a chip off the old block.

Before his mother got ill, she tried to teach him to swim. She stood waist deep in the turquoise cube at the British Club and beckoned to him. But she looked strange with her blonde hair hidden under white rubber flowers and her eyes stretched sideways. Sarah was in the pool and swam underwater from one side to the other and back without breathing. Beyond the chairs and sun-loungers were trees like giant pineapples and a bar where all the fathers stood about drinking beer. Johnny wanted to know what they were laughing at. In the end his mother gave up, and a week later she was flown home, to the Tropical Diseases Hospital in London. And they had only been here a month. That's what happens, his father said, when you forget to take your Paludrin.

The servant is looking at him. Worse, he is speaking. He is saying something like, hey child why you not want to go. Johnny looks down at his feet. The servant crouches down. Johnny breathes through his mouth to avoid smelling the servant's peppery smell. He sees teeth close to, African teeth that can strip the bark off twigs and chew the twigs until they are white and frayed. He feels the prickly feeling that comes just before he wets himself.

'Can I go into the hut now please,' he says. The servant says,

'When I am a small child, mama throw me in the river.'

'Oh,' says the boy.

'Mama want to make boy strong,' says the servant. 'The water go in my nose, and I am frighten. But the sea spirit, she help me. The sea spirit, she see all her little fishes. She spy through all the puddles and rivers, all the oceans and water taps to keep her little fishes safe.'

At last the servant stops talking and Johnny is released. He runs as fast as he can along the beach, flinging his arms and legs around in the way he has been told not to. There is no such thing as a sea spirit. There is just the sea, creeping up the sand, then sucking itself back. As he watches, out of the corner of his eye, he shudders. Each time it moves, it swallows a little more of the beach.

He bends to pick up a shell then throws it down. It's a minor shell, not like his father's shells, stored in a special tin from his travels before Johnny was born. His father is a mechanic and looks after the Land Rovers. Land Rovers have driven me all over the world, he tells him. Johnny runs again, across the hummocky sand towards the monkey trees. They are very tall. The gangs of monkeys are halfway to the sky and the more he looks, the more monkeys there are.

Things are glinting beneath the trees. They look like pieces of water but close to, he sees they are pieces of sky. Next to them is a sunglass lens dented with tooth marks and a camera film sprawling out of a yellow canister. Three teaspoons poke up at different angles and on a torn-off book cover, a black man points at a blackboard. *Times Tables for African Schools*.

Then he sees the spiral shell. It's a monster, even compared to the ones in his father's tin. It's bright white like chalk and covered in blunt knobbly spines. He's scared to pick it up, in case something slimy comes out. It is heavy but very clean. He peers into it then pokes his finger down its pink satin path. His finger can go no further than his eye.

Back at the hut, the other father tells him it's a whopper of a conch and no mistake. The servant says, 'Plenty good shell, plenty clever boy.' When the father has gone, the servant asks whether it's a present for the sea spirit. Johnny clutches the shell to his stomach.

'When the sea spirit see this shell,' says the servant, 'she play on her big trumpet. She let the young master swim all the way back to England, first class, back to mama.' A tear from Johnny's eye pricks the sand, but he stands on it before the servant can see.

They eat stew in the beach hut's main room, their glasses wobbling on the raffia table. The kitchen is a sink and a stove out back under a cane shelter.

'Eat up, Johnny,' says the mother, 'you've only had half.' A lump of gristle goes round and round in his mouth like a giant bogey. Sarah has picked all the pearl barley out and laid it around the edge of her plate like teeth.

'But she's not eating hers,' says Johnny.

'Girls don't eat as much as boys,' says Sarah, 'and anyway, you've got to be a good boy.'

'Children, children,' says Sarah's mother, 'not at the table please.'

Later in bed, he hears the parents talking through the bamboo wall. Their voices are low, but odd words come through. Malaria, he hears, then coma. He covers his head with the pillow.

Later again, his eyes snap open from a dream in which

someone whispers his name. He stares across the room to Sarah's bed. He stares for a long time but she doesn't move. The room is light, but not with daylight. It is the African moon, he thinks, shining through the straw. He peeps out through a gap and gasps. Someone is standing outside, a shape cut out of moonlight. He hears his name again, a squeaky whisper. He glances to where Sarah sleeps. 'What do you want,' he whispers. I' am the sea spirit,' says the voice. 'They tell me there is a boy here, a plenty clever boy.'

Johnny gets out of bed and clambers into his shorts. He stands in the doorway. Ahead, the sea is sparkling ink. He sees a skirt, recognizes the spots. It belongs to Sarah's mother: she wears it at school assembly. A pearly comb (also hers) pokes up from tight curls. Johnny claps his hand over his mouth.

'Come. I am here one night only in the light of the full moon,' says the sea spirit. Johnny's heart races. He looks back at Sarah, wondering why she isn't awake too. The spirit says, 'The girl and the mama-fadder, they will no wake. I make a spell.' The boy does not believe in spells. But his eyes widen anyway.

Outside, everything is different from the day. It's cool. The sea, the sand, the long grass, the trees where the monkeys sleep, perhaps hanging by their tails, are black and white like on TV. The sea spirit puts a finger to her lips and walks in an exaggerated tiptoe towards the sea. The hem of the skirt drags along the sand and the boy fights a wild giggle.

Under his feet, dry sand becomes damp sand. The sea spirit leads him right up to the edge of the sea, where the moon's bright pathway starts. And there is the spiral shell. She must have stolen it and put it there. He wants to protest but doesn't dare. The sea spirit crouches by the shell. A wave wets the hem of her skirt. The boy stands back so the waters don't touch his feet. He wonders if the skirt will get damaged and what the mother will say tomorrow.

The sea spirit takes his hand. Her hand is warm and rough. In front of them the dark sea reels and unreels. 'This biggest shell in Africa,' she says. 'He who done find this shell, the ocean can be him home.' Her eyes are tin foil, like fishes' eyes. She draws a boat in the sand, with a mast, a sail, a pennant. The waters race suddenly towards the boat and rub it out. Johnny tries to step back but she holds him firm and the wave rushes around his toes. The sea is warmer than he expected but even so he can hardly breathe. As it pulls back towards the sea, something gives under his feet and he thinks he will fall backwards. He throws his arms around the sea spirit; feels warmth all down the front of his shorts.

He clutches her while three more waves come and go. He has to try, very hard, not to cry. But before the fourth wave, when she edges him closer to the sea, he doesn't resist.

They are in the sea now, the water surging from Johnny's ankles up to his calves then falling again. But it is not so bad. The sand helps by turning into an anchor around his feet. He relaxes his grip on the sea spirit.

He knows what has to happen. When the next wave comes, he has to let go of the sea spirit. And he does. The warm sea drives into his thighs, drags his calves on its way back out. Johnny stands secure. The pearl comb must have fallen because he sees it bobbing a little way out, on its way back to England, perhaps.

He takes another step forward in preparation for the next wave. When it comes and washes almost up to his waist, cleaning his wetted shorts, he turns to share his delight.

The sea spirit has gone. He gasps and scans the beach in both directions but she has left no sign. He turns back to the sea, black and wrinkled; to the huge white moon. Perhaps she went back under the waves. He knows that's a stupid idea, but he can't help thinking it.

Making Up the Cable

Jim made his way along the pavement, swapping from a stoop to a crouch then back again when his calves complained. The night swirled and fuzzy yellow balls hung above. Where the prison ought to be was nicotine white. It was a relief. Office space was cheap here, but the high buttressed wall that was his daily view made him feel confined, even from the outside. People had been executed there until recently.

He rolled the tape around the wires. They stretched into a distance he couldn't see. A silver half-moon full of Dewar's White Label swung in his inside pocket. Something was making his back teeth ache; a shred of bacon, probably, and his tongue tested the spot continually.

He told his tongue to stop. But a second later it probed again.

The fog took his hearing as well as his sight. A colleague was somewhere along the quarter mile, cutting the pairs of wires to make the take-outs, but far or near, Jim had no idea. And the fog elevated the moisture levels. The cable wouldn't be dry. Every time he thought about it, irritation swarmed inside him. But perhaps it didn't matter. The cable was destined for a mangrove swamp where the atmosphere was one hundred per cent humidity. As was he and the rest of the crew. They'd be on a plane this time next week, now management had brought the trip forward.

Out of the white, a dark figure coalesced.

'Christ,' said Jim.

'Is everything in order here, sir?' The policeman's helmet strap divided his fleshy chin.

Jim laid the roll of tape on the pavement, sticky side up, and stood up.

'Far as I know,' he said. His tongue poked at the rogue sliver.

The policeman turned to his walkie-talkie to say, 'Caledonian Road, near the Ville.' Then he said, 'I'm sure you won't mind explaining, sir, what you're doing in the vicinity of a Category B prison at three o'clock in the morning?'

Sir. Jim had once dined at the Dorchester hotel in Hyde Park and had been impressed by the amount of mockery the head waiter had managed to cram into that word, considering it only had one syllable. The police officer ran him a close second.

The best response would have been friendly. But Jim's words came out in a different tone. 'Goodness, is it that time already? I went home for dinner; must have taken my watch off to do the washing up.'

The officer folded his arms. His silver buttons curved upwards. Droplets of cold water condensed; ran down the back of Jim's neck. He tried for a better tone. 'It's all been cleared, officer,' he said. 'Our management has been in touch with Scotland Yard.' He hoped they had.

The policeman's face remained inert. The fog churned and Jim said that his firm was authorised to use this particular stretch of pavement outside the prison between one and five in the morning. He tried to slide his little fingernail between his back teeth. He remembered the name Inspector Peters. But the policeman said Inspector Peters had left the Force and that he would have to corroborate Jim's version of events with the common-or-garden duty sergeant, if that was good enough for Jim.

Jim said that any delay now was out of the question; that they had to be off the pavement by the time the shift workers started at the bus factory. He picked up the roll of tape, the policeman held up a hand to stop him, and then it was only too easy to call the policeman an officious idiot.

The cell stank of disinfectant. Jim and the man he was hand-cuffed to sat on a thin mattress. Mattress and pillow were covered in a dull red rubber sheeting that reminded Jim of lying in a row with other boys, watching the white enamel bowl full of bloody tonsils approach and waiting for a cloth that would smell appallingly sweet when it was placed over his nose and mouth.

Tipper was stringy, sweating. He had three words tattooed on his forehead, unreadable unless you wanted to stare. Jim didn't.

Tipper's leg jiggled. 'They'll be jittered if I'm not home by day-break,' he said, 'they'll shit all over.' When he'd been registered, Jim noticed, he'd had no wallet, no watch, no belt: nothing for the coppers to confiscate.

Jim, by contrast, had been laden with possessions. 'I'm not a danger to society,' he'd shouted when they'd taken his bag of licorice allsorts, his flask, his shoelaces. 'I'm not a criminal. I'm not bloody Ronnie Biggs.'

'We'll be the judge of that, sir,' the duty officer had said. 'Be-ing drunk and disorderly is a public-order offence.'

'I'm not drunk,' Jim yelled. 'I've had a couple of nips, that's all. It's a cold night.' But the officer made him take his shoes off and turn his socks inside out.

That must have been an hour ago now. Jim didn't know which police station they were in. The journey in the van had taken about twenty minutes.

'This is never a double cell,' said Tipper. 'You couldn't swing a cat in here. And I shouldn't be in here. I was stood there waiting for me mate, I told them. And what about me birds? They'll shit all over, I'm telling you.'

'The coppers can't keep us in here forever,' said Jim.

'Takes them birds days to settle once they get spooked,' said Tipper. 'Once they start messing everywhere, whole loft'll need chloroxing.'

Further down the row, someone banged the bars and yelled.

Jim wondered if his work colleague knew what had happened to him. The police didn't seem to believe that his colleague existed, so perhaps nobody had told him.

He dug his little fingernail between his back teeth. His right hand was handcuffed to Tipper's so he had to use his left. He tasted salt and metal.

At least Maureen was a hundred miles away in Gloucester. She was saying goodbye to her mother; had taken their daughter down from Victoria. Tomorrow she'd go to the Cross, buy mosquito nets, iodine, tomato ketchup.

'Them Jacobins is the worst,' said Tipper. 'They get ornery. You have to put pine needles down for them special.' His voice was fond. 'Them birds is the same as human beings. They feels things.'

Jim massaged his cheek.

'Got the toothache have you,' said Tipper.

Jim was startled. 'It's nothing,' he said. Water seeped out of his right eye.

Tipper grinned. His own teeth were mostly missing.

'I've got a bit of food lodged,' said Jim.

'Here,' said Tipper. 'I might have something.'

Jim had a moment of wild hope. Perhaps it was something drinkable.

But Tipper took off one of his slip-ons. They were scuffed, black.

'You've come to the right person,' he said, as he turned the shoe over. The sole was very worn; had a small hole at the ball. 'I have to do bits and bobs for me birds, see, sorting out their beaks and that. Lucky I've got me right hand free.' Holding the shoe between his thighs, he pulled the heel off. 'Take a tip. The Plod might look *in* yer shoes but they never looks *inside* of them.'

In the heel compartment was a miniature Swiss Army knife. Tipper took it out and wiped it on his sleeve. He fanned out implements: corkscrew, scissors, file.

'It's decent of you,' said Jim. 'But...'

'I know what you're thinking,' said Tipper. 'But there's a sight more germs in your mouth, son, than there is in my shoe.'

He advanced quickly. There was the sight of another man's eyebrows close-up, a smell like drains, a second of sharp pain, then Tipper was saying 'got the bastard'. He sniffed. 'Been in there a day or two, I reckon,' he said.

The relief of pressure was profound. Jim worked his jaw, ran his tongue over his teeth.

'Better,' said Tipper.

'Yeah,' said Jim.

Tipper grinned.

Jim was about to thank him, when a thought crossed his mind. He frowned.

Tipper folded the knife, placed it back in its dark chamber. He tapped the heel gently on the floor to secure the tacks.

'All right, mate?' he asked Jim.

Jim grunted.

There was a pause.

'Cause you must be feeling scads better,' said Tipper, 'now

I've got that little tinker out for you.'

Jim shrugged.

'Only, I thought you'd be made up,' said Tipper. His tone was plaintive.

Jim didn't reply. His mind was busy conjuring all the possible favours a man like Tipper might want him to do in return.

Tipper was talking on, his voice a whine. The Jacobins, the Plod, the way society was going, the way no-one said thank you anymore, not even when you put yourself out to help a virtual bloody stranger. No-one asked you to do it – you just did it out of the goodness of your own heart.

But Jim had sunk into a dark world of his own. He didn't speak, just sat with his back against the cold cell wall, waiting.

The Prodigal Son

When he finally gave up drinking, my father received a gift from God. He lives in a tiny ground floor flat by the sea, and evidence of his gift now fills the loft and ousts clothes and crockery from the wardrobe and cupboards.

I walk down the communal corridor, hung with bland corporate paintings of flowers and fruit. He leaves the door on the latch when I'm due and it's a worry. Rogues abound in this town. He should know – he used to be one of them. Empty hotels became halfway houses for men fresh from Armley, Wealstun, Full Sutton. Not that Dad was ever inside. He avoided that – just.

I open the door to the smell of TCP and toilet bowl.

'Hello Dad,' I shout but have to touch his arm before he turns from the kitchenette, where he's spooning instant coffee into two china beakers in readiness.

'Hello love.' He grins, his mouth a cave. His denture is by the kettle, pink as chewed bubblegum. He has shaved for me, and his face is pink from scrubbing.

Braces hold up mud-coloured trousers. His short sleeves are frayed. He makes summer shirts from winter ones in a few seconds with the kitchen scissors. My mother still buys him three long-sleeved ones in every January sale, though they divorced decades ago. He wears them till April; then the scissors come out.

He puts the mugs on a little tray. He crosses the room by grabbing the backs of armchairs, and the tray tilts and wobbles but I know not to offer help. It touches down on the coffee table and he topples into his chair. 'Oh boy,' he says.

I sit down too. 'How are you doing, Dad?'

'Sorry?' he says, groping for his Rothmans and lighting up. His freckled shins shine above the soft woollen rolls of his socks, elastic tops snipped off. Smoke streams from his nose.

'Cheers,' he says, as we raise scalding weak coffee to our lips. 'Now, you were saying?'

'Just wondering how you've been getting on, Dad,' I shout.

The blander my utterances, the more inane they sound repeated. But Dad has given up on his hearing aid. God transmits His will to the inner ear, not the outer one.

He nods. 'Not bad,' he says. 'Though outwardly we are wasting away, yet inwardly we are renewed, day by day.' His wink doesn't quell my unease. I'll never get used to his new language.

'What sort of a week have *you* had?' he asks.

It has been a week from hell at the hospital, but I don't tell him that. 'Fine,' I say.

'I expect you've been watching the tennis,' he says.

The world of work no longer exists for him, if it ever really did, so much of it lost to blackouts and hangovers. I wonder which tournament's on. Wimbledon? Queens?

'How's Andy Murray doing?' I ask.

That's a safe bet.

'Sorry?' He cups his hands round his ears.

'I said, has Andy Murray got through?'

'Knocked out in the third round,' he says. 'Played like an arse.' I glimpse the old Dad, constantly aghast at other people's idiocy. 'Oh well, I don't suppose it matters much. Blessed is the man who remains steadfast under trial.' He smiles: he's making an effort.

I ask about the Residents Association, then about the new local supermarket. He waves these subjects away. I'm not scoring.

'What about the Russians?' I try. 'Any sign lately?'

He shakes his head.

Fair enough. With some topics you can't go in cold.

We sit in silence.

There's another subject, one I've been putting off. I brace myself. 'Did you finish the ballroom scene?' I ask.

'Ah,' he says, 'now you're talking. Hang on a minute.'

He pulls a canvas out from under his chair.

Painting came to my father at two in the morning, when the Lord moved him to rise and turn on the television. On screen was an actress he recognised, from a situation comedy he'd once loved. He watched the show – a painting competition – and later, bleary in the art shop, identified the acrylic paints used by the winner. God's preferred subject matter was revealed at the library, where a display of art books featured the works of Tissot.

'But you've never painted before,' I said at the time. 'You've taken no interest in art.'

My father raised his eyes to the sky. 'Remember not the former things,' he said, 'nor consider the things of old. Behold, I am doing a new thing; now it springs forth, do you not perceive it? I will make a way in the wilderness and rivers in the desert.'

His tone was irony free.

That was two years ago. Now we gaze on a nineteenth-century ballroom scene. Dark-suited musicians surround a piano. A polished floor sweeps forward to a group of guests chatting, their heads oversized, their fingers bunched like bananas, their eyes lurid, their feet poking out at right angles to their legs.

God blessed my father with an ability to render furniture and buildings: people are another matter.

'You've captured the reflection of the light on the dark wood,' I say.

'Sorry?'

'You've got the shine just right,' I yell. 'On the floorboards.'

He beams. 'Tell you what – it's a while since you've seen them laid out together. I expect you could do with a refresher.'

I saw them last week, and the week before last. But I nod.

He shuffles to the sideboard, pulls out paintings. He keeps them hidden, because of the Russians. In the kitchenette, he props four on the work surface, two on the fridge and one on the cooker. One balances on the sink taps. Finally we're surrounded by a crowd in top hats and naval caps; long gloves and frilly, colourful gowns. Fans abound. Necks are stiff, mouths are large and small and limbs are oddly jointed. It's like being in a nightmare. The tap drips under a group of picnickers.

'You've done so much work,' I say.

'I can do all things through Him who strengthens me,' says my father.

A tear runs down his cheek. I'm startled and don't know what to say.

'Have you a favourite?' he asks, a catch in his voice.

'I like them all,' I say, almost meaning it. 'The colours are atmospheric; the storytelling is charming.'

He picks up 'The Prodigal Son.' While sailors unload a ship in the background, a young man kneels on a wet walkway to clasp an older man around the waist. The old man's top hat is tumbling.

'You've always liked this one,' he says. 'Go on, it's yours.'

I'm taken aback. 'Wouldn't it be better to keep them together as a collection?' I say.

'I thought that at first,' he said. 'But haven't you noticed, one's already gone.'

I glance quickly around. '"The Party on the Ship"?' I say. '"The Lady Surrounded by Autumn Leaves"?'

'No,' he says. 'Sit down and I'll tell you.'

We weave back to the chairs.

'Tell me which one's gone,' I say. 'And who you gave it to.'

'Gave? Gave? I sold it,' he says, lighting another cigarette. 'As good as.'

My mouth hangs open.

He tells me the story, smoke jerking from his mouth. Last week he had an extraction. He's hung on to his last brown teeth, battling the dentist, who he calls the Greek. Rotten teeth cause heart problems, said the Greek. Rubbish, said my father. You'd want to keep yours if you only had four left.

'Does it hurt?' I ask.

'Irrelevant,' he says. 'The point is I struck a deal. The Greek tried to charge me fifty-four quid when it only took him a minute to pull it out. Could've done it myself with a bit of string if there was a door in this place I could slam.' He jabs a finger. 'Bloody dampers, bloody health and safety.'

He goes on. 'Anyway, I told him about my paintings. This place could do with brightening up, I said to him. Tell you what – as a favour – I said, I'll let you have one for fifty-four quid.'

'And he took it?' I say.

My father narrows his eyes. I hope I didn't sound astonished. 'Damn right he took it,' he says. 'Those Greeks know a bargain when they see one.'

'Did he come here?' I ask, imagining a dark-bearded man in a white coat stroking his chin among my father's pots and pans.

'Of course not,' says my father. 'He's a busy man. I took a few over, gave him a choice. He picked "Young Lady in a Boat". Not my best. But then, the Greeks never knew much about art.'

I struggle not to contest that. But arguing with my father, drunk or sober, is pointless. I hope the Greek remembers to put the painting up when Dad goes for his checkups.

My father talks on. I half listen. I'm thinking about black olives and green sea.

'Oh well,' he says, 'I don't suppose any of it matters much.'

We reflect on that.

'There's some big tankers on the horizon today,' I say. 'I saw them on the way in.'

'Yes,' says my father, rallying again. 'And I know what they're up to.' He taps his nose. 'When I go out for my walk I see the light glinting off their binoculars.'

Dad's windows face away from the sea. He keeps his own binoculars on the windowsill, anyway.

'One's an aircraft carrier,' he says. 'Admiral Kuznetsov. There's a whole fleet on their way down to the British Channel. The Royal Navy needs to get a shift on, send some destroyers. Those boys need shadowing.'

I wonder where he got the name of the carrier. From his own distant years in the navy, perhaps.

'Do you think they're a threat?'

He glares. 'Of course they're a threat. Have you forgotten the Cold War?'

To be honest, I had. I make a non-commital sound.

'The Lord trieth the righteous,' says my father, 'but the wicked and him that loveth violence his soul hateth.'

'Do you think they're after your paintings?' I ask. He grunts. 'They might raise a few bob back in Russia. Make it onto the walls of the State Gallery in Moscow.'

My former father could laugh at himself until the tears ran. But my new father is different. 'Why do you think I keep them under wraps,' he says. 'Why do you think I don't hang them?'

'There's walls between you and the sea,' I say. 'The Russians couldn't see your paintings if they tried.'

'They have infrared technology now,' says my father. 'Radar scanners. They can see through walls using microwaves. Then there's the Doppler shift. Oh, never underestimate the Russians. They got Yuri Gagarin into space in 1961. Left the Americans standing.'

Once a scientist, always a scientist. You can't discount what he says.

I hear the ping of a text. In my handbag, my screen is lit with a picture of Tumfy the cat, a reminder of my world. It's half past five. It's a long drive home and I'm meeting a friend for a drink first.

'I suppose I'd better go, Dad,' I say. I hate saying it. Days go by when my father doesn't speak to anyone but God; when his voice goes rusty.

'I'm meeting Jenny at six,' I add, 'in one of the harbour pubs. From school days, remember?'

He frowns. 'Jenny,' he says. 'What did her father do?'

'He worked at Tate and Lyle,' I say. 'In Liverpool.'

'Tall chap with square glasses,' says my father. 'Bit of a boffin.'

'I suppose so,' I say. 'But anyway, Jenny's an academic now.

At Hull. She publishes books on Philip Larkin. They're highly regarded.'

'Oh,' says my father, uninterested.

'Anyway,' I say, 'I'd best be off.'

My father nods and grips the arms of his chair. He begins the business of standing.

'Look after yourself,' I say. 'I'll see you next week.'

He waves from the open door. I walk down the corridor and step out into the air. I'm heartsick; I'm saved. The world is full of movement.

A jar of greyish pickled eggs stands on the pub bar. Muzak bubbles from fruit machines; the ceiling is low, the carpeting red. My friend bags a bench in a dark nook while I go for the drinks. Perhaps I'll tell her about my father, perhaps not.

A group of men drink shots at the bar. 'Two white wine spritzers,' I shout above their heads.

'What's a spritzer,' asks the barman.

'White wine and soda,' I yell.

One of the men glances at me; says something to the others in a foreign language. They laugh but their attention turns quickly back to a device one of them holds, like a gun with a screen on it.

While the barman searches for wine, I peer through a gap between backs.

On the screen is a photo of a painting, picked out in the bright colours of thermal imaging: yellow, green, orange. I can't be sure, but it looks like a young man kneeling on a dockside walkway. He's embracing an older man. The older man's top hat is tumbling to the ground.

I Love Tea

The three women stood outside the front door, hunched against the sea breeze. As they leant towards each other, a lighter glinted in the sun. One of them hadn't smoked for nearly a year but today was different. They gazed downhill to where the suicide bridge sectioned the sea into four. Their faces were landslides of disappointment, held back by foundation, faint hope, fixed smiles; lines led to their mouths. The town was beautiful, with a ruined castle. It was also full of people trying to go straight and hotels no-one could afford to refurbish.

'Fourth time I've been through this,' said one, 'can you believe it?' She peered through the door, which was glass. 'Come on, come on, I've enough on my plate as it is.'

The wind blew ash into the rose bushes.

'How long is it this time?' the second one asked.

'Six month,' said the first. 'He should've been discharged weeks ago. But they never seem to think he's ready. Haven't seen you here before, love.'

'No,' said the third, the youngest. She was trying to take in the news that once might not be enough. The others tilted towards her. She thought about telling the story, but couldn't muster the enthusiasm.

'Is it men-only?' she offered.

Smoke came down the woman's nostrils in bursts.

'At present, yeah. Women have got more sense. Most of the time.'

A man arrived at the other side of the door. The women ground their cigarettes into the path.

'Are you alright love?' said the first one.

'Yeah,' said the third. Whatever happened in there, she was not going to cry. Not in front of strangers. That was what she told herself, though in fact crying in front of family or friends would have been worse.

The sea glittered in the distance.

The scuffed leather-look sofas in the sitting room had been sat in by too many people. Even the window glass was brown. Scuffed leather-look men rose to greet the stream of people that were suddenly there, laughing and joking. Hardened visitors.

But he wasn't there.

The man on the phone, Barry, had said a visit was a good idea. Saturday, from twelve onwards, he'd said, and I'll tell him you're coming. It was her weekend off, had seemed meant to be. Not that time off was a problem these days when all anyone talked about was work/life balance, outside interests, family. Though where you were supposed to get them from, no-one said.

One of the men, on a sofa by the window, hadn't moved. His nose looked like an internal organ migrated to the outside, his clothes barely occupied. A sign above his head stated 'GOD. Good Orderly Direction.'

She would ask him if he knew a Jim.

He got to his feet. His trousers were smeared in ash and his mustard cardigan seemed to have bullet holes. Behind him, flesh-coloured roses walloped the window.

'Didn't recognise me, did you,' he said.

His voice was filtered through an old man's quaver. His eyes were red rimmed, infected looking, but she made herself meet them. She leant towards him, holding her breath in case he smelt of piss.

It must be ten years. She'd stood on the doorstep of a Victorian building converted to flats and found his name under a plastic cover. A Mr without a Mrs. She climbed lino stairs to his bed-sit, saw orange skirting-board, brown nylon carpet, furniture assembled from different decades. If he had been a student, it would have been okay.

Ebony elephants trudged across the mantelpiece, one tusk between them. They looked so out of place she had to excuse herself down the corridor to the bathroom and sit on the edge of the bath, swallowing and swallowing again.

When she went back, they drank tea out of flowered mugs which had grown a tunnel of brown rings. She had known there must have been something to talk about besides the dog. The fleshy middle-aged men in bomber jackets, perhaps, who banged on her mother's door demanding money, or the way she wouldn't give them his new address.

She didn't visit again. He made no effort to keep in touch either but then he never had; it was her mother who had always done the phoning, sent the cards, suggested the meet-ups.

Now he was nodding at a hatch on the other side of the room, a kettle, a clutch of mugs. 'Want one?' he asked.

'Alright.'

Each step he took away from her was a balm. She shouldn't be here, should have thrown away that number; stopped the story spooling from her mother's mouth.

Hopeless men shuffled around the hatch, dropping things.

Spoons rattled against jars as they tried to scoop coffee, helped by a young man with blue arms who wore a PVC apron with a picture of a bra and suspenders. The woman who'd spoken to her outside, who'd seemed so tough, sat across the room pressing a tissue to her eyes as if trying to stop them falling out. Those cards were all over the walls. 'Thy Will Not My Will.' 'KISS. Keep it Simple, Stupid.'

He came back carrying two huge white mugs. He walked as if edging around something. 'The fuckers took all the hot water.'

Her pulse quickened at the swear word. He'd never used language like that.

Her mug said 'I Love Tea' and a pale corner poked out. He'd brought no spoon so she fished at the bag with her finger nails, squeezed it against the side of the mug, scalding herself. She dumped it in an ashtray. Cigarette butts swam, some of them smoked so hard that the filter showed dark pinpricks.

'The tea's a bit basic,' he said.

'I suppose the whole place is,' she said.

He shrugged. She wondered what kind of life he'd been leading since she last saw him.

'Is it Christian?' she asked.

He swigged his tea. 'Spiritual. One of their words. God knows what it means.'

He fumbled a pack of cigs from his cardigan pocket, unwound cellophane. The logo on the pack was silver and purple.

He saw her looking. 'Yeh,' he said, 'Silkies. Like smoking air. But what can you do?'

'How does it work here?'

'Who said it works?'

'You look well.'

'Even I know I look bloody awful.' He tapped ash onto ash. 'We could get out of here, if you like, get some fresh air. It's a couple of hours till the meeting.'

What meeting, she thought. And was he allowed out? She stared at him.

He smiled, after a fashion. 'Don't get your knickers in a twist, it's kosher.'

The woman across the room was openly crying now, the man in the apron comforting her. He looked used to comforting people.

'Who's that man?' she asked.

'Oh, that's Tom. He hasn't got much between the ears.'

Luckily, Tom was out of earshot.

Jim returned to his subject. 'Got to have a chaperone, y'see.'

He waved his cigarette around; knocked the ashtray off the chair arm. Slurry and fag ends sprayed across the carpet but he didn't seem to notice. Neither did the carpet.

'Don't trust you as far as they can throw you,' he said.

When he spoke about 'them' it was with grim cheer.

'Who's your chaperone normally?'

'Anyone who's been in the programme longer than me. Which is just about anyone. Suppose they're not a bad bunch.'

He eyed her. 'Or we can just forget it. Stay here. Drink tea till we puke our guts out.'

She stood up.

They went upstairs to get his jacket. His door, which he said he wasn't allowed to close with a visitor inside, opened onto two single beds with frilly lemon counterpanes. Dumbbells stood by the wall, a picture of a wife and kids on a bedside cabinet.

'You've got a roommate,' she said.

'Spends half the night shouting,' he said, 'or else jumping up and down doing his fucking keep fit.'

On the beach, the striped windbreaks slapped and heaved. Children ran about, donkeys slogged along parallel to the water and a few people shrieked in the sea. On doughnut stands, rings of batter bobbed in oil then were pulled up a little slope and dumped in sugar.

They descended stone steps to the sand. He kicked sand onto people's towels, clipped their sandcastles. He lit one cigarette from the butt of another. At the water's edge, the waves clamoured and no matter how many times she said she couldn't hear, he kept saying things. Ahead, the donkeys turned and began to trudge back. She wished they would break into a gallop.

He hurled a pebble across the waves. Once, he'd been a young man in shorts and sandals with a crew cut, and she'd stood in her yellow cotton dress watching his pebble skip five times across a warm brown sea that barely moved. Now, his pebble disappeared into the froth. He didn't acknowledge it. Bloody rubbish, she imagined him thinking.

In the cafe, clutches of squeezy plastic bottles, spouts encrusted with yellow, brown and red, stood on every table.

Jim queued at the counter. 'I've ordered us a couple of soups, tomato, all right?'

The soups arrived with parsley perched on top like pond insects. Jim stirred a spoonful of sugar into his. His hand shook and grains span across the table. He had already emptied half the canister into his tea and sprinkled sugar on his bread.

He slurped his soup and the white bread went round and round in his mouth. The table was too small. He began telling her about the meetings, the regime, the other men. He had always been one for grumbling and blaming. She hadn't deluded herself that he'd want to talk about the past but now she realised there was a limit to how much she wanted to hear about his present. She was deliriously grateful when he got up to queue for two more steaming polystyrene cups.

Then it all began again. While he was talking, he picked his nose, his ear, his chin. Removed bits, examined them between his fingers, flicked them onto the floor.

Back in the brown sitting room, layers of smoke hung like chiffon scarves. They headed for the sofa again. The clock told her that in ten minutes she would have been here for two hours. She craved the long anonymous roads, but she would wait the last minutes out, using the same discipline that enabled her to pour one unit of wine into a glass and the rest down the sink.

As she was formulating her goodbye, Tom came in with a clipboard.

Jim looked at her with a plea in his eyes.

Somehow she allowed people to draw hard chairs up and form a circle that included her.

The meeting began with a minute's silence then a welcome for the two guests who were left. A theme was announced: gratitude. A baton worked its way around the room and you were allowed to speak only when you held it. Rules seemed to underpin the way people spoke, and certain phrases cropped up too much. She dreaded hearing Jim speak but when his turn came, he passed and she burned with shame. A man with a livid pink scalp said life was hard work when you didn't feel at home in your own skin. Because of what had happened to his son, he'd lost many years to anger. The one thing he was grateful for today was his wife. He turned to the tough woman who'd cried. 'Thank you,' he said. 'Every time you visit me, you travel a lot further than fifty miles.'

The men nodded and mumbled, and Jim's eyes shone with tears. The woman stared at the floor. The hour went on, long and earnest, and ended in a welter of bonhomie.

Sarah realised that she'd made it through. She tried for a smile. 'Okay,' she said. 'And now I really do have to go.'

Jim nodded.

A voice rose over the din. 'Who knocked this lot over?'

Tom was pointing to a mess of trodden in cigarette ends on the carpet. She waited for her father to own up.

Tom went to the hatch and came back with a dustpan and brush. He stood over the patch again. 'I said who spilt this?'

'Dad,' she whispered. 'I think it was you.'

'Uh?'

'You knocked it over. Before we went out.'

He looked blank. But Tom had noticed. Perhaps he already knew. 'Well, here's a dustpan and brush,' he said to Jim. 'The rest is your responsibility.' He went back over to the hatch.

Jim shrugged and lit another cigarette. Elsewhere in the room, conversations resumed.

It wasn't worth an argument, not when they'd managed to avoid one all day.

'I'll do it,' she said.

She went down on her hands and knees and tried to brush the carpet. Some of the mess was wet, some dry. What ash she managed to disturb rose in a soft, choking cloud.

She sensed someone above her.

It was her instinct to cower. But it was only Tom, holding his hand out for the dustpan. She gave it to him and he helped her to her feet. He was younger than she was but he brushed ash from the knees of her jeans in the brisk, capable way a father might, and she stood there letting him. Then he tipped her sweepings back onto the carpet and handed the dustpan and brush to Jim.

She stared. She waited for her father to say that no fat-necked barrow boy was going to tell him what to do.

But Jim began to lower himself to his knees, gingerly, like someone getting down to pray.

She thought she was going to cry. She shot a quick look around the room, daring anyone to laugh or throw a pitying look. But no-one was looking, except the tough woman, who gave a half smile and rolled her eyes as if this was the latest scene in a soap opera that stretched credulity.

Jim pressed the brush bristles into the sour carpet and succeeded in transferring a tiny amount of ash to the pan. Then he did it again.

She found her voice. 'What if he can't get up?'

'Oh, he'll get up,' said Tom.

It dawned on her that this was funny; in fact, chokingly funny.

And suddenly she was laughing and then weeping, in the roomful of strangers. And Tom was putting his arms around her as if this was all in a day's work, and she was turning into him and hiccupping and gasping, her tears running down his joke apron.

Mobylette Dreams

The *Lycée général et technologique* was like a vast aquarium. No burnished floorboards or jammed sash windows; no gloomy stairs. Everything was white, even the blackboards. A greaseball in a jeans jacket, not Lindsey's idea of a teacher, covered one with blue marker pen and told the group that here was ze list of study pairs; that zey must help one an udder.

All over the room, eyes were caught and places changed but the girl who was meant to be Lindsey's partner got up and walked out. Lindsey glanced around for help but everyone's gaze span away from her, ice across a frozen pond. Then a tidal wave of French students crashed in, making chairs fall and tables scream, and French History began. 'Marie-Antoinette', 'Bastille' and 'guillotine' were the only words Lindsey understood. She might have understood more had the girls not been knitting and eating pink meat sandwiches, the boys not teetering on the back legs of chairs.

When she left the Lycée gates at lunchtime, her partner fell in beside her.

'Where have you been?' Lindsey asked, trying not to cry.

'Nowhere,' said Sarah.

Sarah had long bare legs and had spent the train journey to France knotted with a boy in the corner. Also, she wore a bra. Lindsey had woken that morning in their windowless breezeblock room and seen Christ looking down on it from his mahogany cross.

'But we're meant to be helping each other,' said Lindsey. It was drizzling, but something made her keep her Minnie Mouse umbrella in her bag.

Sarah's eyes grazed a shop window, with its green and white boxes of anti-cellulite cream.

'Don't tell me you've fallen for that study pairs crap. They're only doing that so's they can get away without teaching us anything.' Before Lindsey could ask why she was suddenly so keen on learning, she said, 'Anyway, why are you so impressed with everything? It's only *France*.'

Sarah, Lindsey already knew, had lived in Nigeria as a child. But for Lindsey, France was enough. Gordon Honeycombe had said on the *News at Ten* the other night that the Seventies was opening up foreign travel to the average Briton. But this was the first time it had happened to her, unless you counted the Isle of White.

Lunch – meat and lettuce – was served at the kitchen table, where a waxed tablecloth bore pictures of dark grapes. The lettuce glistened, only just green. Horse, hissed Sarah, shunting oily gristle across her plate. Lindsey's mother admitted to being a poor cook but Lindsey longed for her tuna and pasta bake that came entirely out of tins.

Madame crossed and re-crossed the black and white check floor, a cornered queen. Her face was an egg, her forearms raw turkey legs in the tight sleeves of her black dress. She'd spoken to them once, when she'd shown them to their room in the garage.

'Is forbidden the boys and also the hairspray.'

Lindsey wanted more. But her carefully phrased French questions hung in the greasy air. Dessert was the 'toasts' that had been there at breakfast. Lindsey already knew they stayed hard and dry, no matter what.

In the garage, squeezing past the red tin car, Sarah said, 'I don't know why you bother. She doesn't want to talk to *us*. Stick to your comics.'

'They're not comics. They're *Asterix the Gaul*.' Sarah looked blank. She was thick, thought Lindsey. 'You can't learn everything from books,' Lindsey added. 'That's why I've come to France. To improve my oral.' Lindsey wondered why Sarah snorted.

Lindsey's bed had a spring base and was bowed like an old nag. Sarah had claimed the divan, hard but horizontal. In the underwater light, Lindsey bounced, making her springs squawk while Sarah applied lip-gloss in the mirror above the wash basin.

'Going somewhere?' asked Lindsey.

Sarah rolled her eyes.

'Your lips look exactly the same as when you started,' said Lindsey. 'I don't know why you bother.'

'Yeah, but they taste different. Not that you'd know anything about why that matters. Can you stop jigging about on that stupid bed?'

Lindsey bounced some more. 'Are you meeting that boy?'

'He's called James, for your information.'

'Well, can we go to the study meeting together later? At the cafe?'

'Like I'm going to that.'

Sarah flung the door open, making a rectangle of light so bright it hurt.

Along with a warning about unpasteurised cheese, Lindsey's mother had given her a map book. The town was squares and lozenges with a few triangles thrown in. Following the map to the cafe, Lindsey felt better, despite the titchy street signs and the traffic lights being too high up and in the wrong order. The sky discharged sun and rain alternately; typical France or typical April? Inside a mesh fence, a black dog ran, the Milky Way on its coat. Outside the Tabac, *Le Monde* had Giscard D'Estaing on the front page.

Pierre began the meeting by taking off his mirror shades and hoisting himself onto a table. He lit a cigarette from a blue pack; Gauloises. All the French smoked them and they stank. Tomorrow, he said, was a coach trip. 'You will travel wiz your study partner. You will work together for zuh day. Is fun activity.'

Students smiled at each other and Lindsey realised that they were all bosom buddies already. Her neck grew hot. Perhaps Miss Grant had been wrong to recommend this trip. Tears were leaking out, so she retreated to the toilet where the mirror confirmed her as a freak. Her seat was taken by a girl in white dungarees. Her duffel coat had gone under the table and she had to scrabble for it. Outside she walked straight into Pierre.

'Ey, ey, ey!' he said, putting out an arm. 'Your nose, he is hurt.'

There was something hot on her top lip. Her fingers came away red and slippery.

'It's alright,' she said. 'I get them. Nose bleeds.'

He dabbed her with his hanky then pressed it into her hand. Formerly beige and blue, it was now carnage. His breath made her eyes water. 'There. I sink you will live.'

He flicked the switch on his Mobylette and climbed onto the pedals. Across the street, a dog came out of a boulangerie. The blood was sticky on Lindsey's fingers.

He looked down. 'Zumzing is ze matter?'

She feared using up all his kindness the way she often did with her mother.

'No? Yes?' he said.

'I'm alright.'

He nodded his approval and zoomed off with a noise like a chainsaw. She walked away from the cafe, in no particular direction.

In the coach drone, Lindsey travelled behind two denim hats that tilted and bobbed. She couldn't hear their conversation, but eventually a hat rotated and a plastic box came between the seat backs. 'Want some chocolate cake?' asked a girl, light glinting off the metalwork in her mouth. 'It's homemade.'

After that, even though they were Scottish and wore knee socks, it would have been mean to ditch them. Their French was tragic but perhaps that was the fault of the Scottish education system. Lindsey helped them identify the Mairie flag, the town square and a statue of a fat man with a telescope.

On the edge of a fountain, they unpacked plump foil parcels and kicked at advancing squads of French pigeons. Lindsey's stomach snarled at the sight of crusty bread and thick ham tongues. The girl with braces eyed Lindsey's toasts and triangles of cheese spread.

'Pierre's coming!' hissed the other. '*She* thinks he's lush,' she told Lindsey.

'I do not!' said the girl with braces, stuffing her sandwich into her bag as if covering up a crime.

'For you clever girls, I have questionnaire number two,' called Pierre. 'You have finished the first, yes?' Lindsey marvelled at all the French people coming and going in the square, oblivious of Pierre and everything he was. He jerked his head. His teeth were brown and white, like tulip bulbs. 'Allo? You can talk, one of you?'

The girl with braces fumbled pages into his hand. 'It was a brewyant questionnaire. The town is brewyant too.'

'Zis place?' said Pierre. 'Is okay for the children and the olds. But the young people sink it – how you say – a shit hole.'

The girls were all mouth and eyes.

'Is bad word?' asked Pierre.

They nodded. He walked away backwards. '*C'est ca*! You will take wiz you home the new English swear words as well as the old French ones.'

He headed for another trio of girls.

'He *winked* at you,' the second girl told Lindsey, eyeing her friend.

In the room that evening, Sarah went to the mirror above the basin and shrieked. 'Ugh, are these your knickers?'

The rust coloured water was from Pierre's hanky. But Lindsey nodded. 'Yeah, I came on earlier today.'

'Information overload,' said Sarah.

She brushed her hair until it was vertical then forced her hairbrush into her jeans pocket. She opened the wardrobe. She had millions of clothes, which she wore in weird combos, like a floaty red dress with black bovva boots, and she had hogged all the hangers. Lindsey's striped rugby shirts and stretch stirrup trousers hunkered on the shelves, shielding Piggy the pyjama case, his flanks plump with two brushed-cotton nighties. Sarah put on a top that looked more like a bra and headed for the door.

'Aren't you taking a bag?'

'Shock, horror. By the way, that teacher is old enough to be your father.'

'What?'

'James saw you. After the meeting. You let him *paw* you. Then you were pleading with him.'

'I was not! I had a nosebleed.'

'Yeah, right. It's sick either way.'

And Sarah was gone.

Later that night, Lindsey was woken by the sound of sobbing. She got out of bed and groped her way to the light switch. Sarah was sitting up, tears running into the neck of her cream silk pyjamas.

'What's happened?' asked Lindsey. 'Has your mum died?'

Sarah clutched her knees and rocked.

She was probably hysterical. When people got hysterical in films, they usually got a slap across the face but Lindsey didn't feel up to doing that. She went over to Sarah's bed and stood chewing her thumb.

'Fucking French,' she made out. 'I hate them. The women are all slags.'

'Is it James?'

Sarah went into fresh seizures of grief. Lindsey had never seen anyone this upset. It was hard to credit a moron with a floppy fringe as the cause.

'It's no use crying over spilt milk,' she managed.

'I'll tell you something else,' said Sarah, blowing her nose on a yard of toilet paper. 'I'll show him.' Sarah cried into her knees.

'What do you mean?' Lindsey lost interest. 'If you're okay

now, I'm going to put the light off and go back to bed.'

'Do I *look* okay?'

But Lindsey went anyway and lay with the pillow over her head. She longed for Piggy but didn't dare fetch him. Even broken hearted, Sarah would probably still dish out ridicule.

In the morning, although she must have heard Lindsey's alarm, a hammer that turned into a blur between two bells, Sarah stayed humped under the covers.

'How about a nice cup of tea?' asked Lindsey.

The hump remained silent.

It was a long morning, thanks to double *education civique, juridique et sociale* and back at the house, Sarah was gone. Lindsey had prepared French lies to cover for her, but Mme didn't ask.

At three, another cafe meeting took place and James was there, wedged into a chair with a dark-haired girl who had hairy armpits.

'Can I take your photo?' Lindsey asked Pierre afterwards.

'Another time, yes?' he said, staring over her shoulder as he mounted his Mobylette. 'I am retarded.'

She took it anyway.

Blank shots remained on the film but she pressed rewind, went to the Pharmacie and ordered the service *exprès*. On the way home, she pushed pieces of dry toast through the fence for the black dog. He wolfed them silently then barked for more. She moved off, afraid the owners would come out and shout in French.

Sarah must surely be back by now. Lindsey was planning an apology. With James out of the way, Sarah might enjoy a game of travel chess. The pieces were small but alright if you knew what they were meant to be. Lindsey also had travel Scrabble, which they could play in French.

She opened the door to an empty room.

Dinner was white fish that had been boiled, perhaps for hours: the windows were fogged. Dessert was dried gooseberries that exploded on the tongue. Both courses came and went without Sarah. Mme was silent and solid as a wardrobe. Lindsey began to worry. When was the appropriate time to report a missing person in France? Which of Sarah's many items of clothing would be best for the sniffer dogs?

Alone back in the room, she spread out the nine coloured squares she'd got from the Pharmacie. All were of Pierre, mirror shades on or off, man-bag present or absent, cigarette lit, unlit or still in the blue packet. In all the shots he was grinning, giving her the thumbs up or winking; except in today's, where he looked distracted.

Lindsey frowned. Then she made a mouth out of her thumb and forefinger and tipped over on the bed, pressing her lips against it.

She didn't know she'd fallen asleep until she woke up. The light was still on and her Baby Ben alarm clock said two-thirty. She had rolled onto the shiny squares in her sleep. She snatched them up. Two were creased but today's shot was okay. As she studied it again, she felt a trickle of fear. When she took the shot, she'd known Pierre was looking at something – or someone – behind her. But now she saw, in the top corner of each mirrored shade a little blob that could have been the reflection of a floaty red dress.

Tears prickled her eyes. She had known in her heart of hearts that nothing would really happen with Pierre. He was too old, and anyway it was probably forbidden by French law. It was sad but bearable. But this was something new. Thinking that she had never felt so lonely in all her life, she fetched Piggy from the wardrobe and lay on top of him, pressing her face into his pink flanks to muffle her sobs. Piggy, however, even stuffed with two nighties, was not substantial enough to offer much comfort and from the depths of despair came an idea that made Lindsey get up and go to the wardrobe.

Sarah's clothes came easily to hand. She emptied her hangers then opened a drawer and pulled out crop tops, bras and knickers; threw them onto Sarah's bed. When all the clothes were out of the wardrobe, she sat down and sorted through them. She selected some white drainpipe jeans and a black shirt with flat mother of pearl buttons sewn on close together all the way up. She laid them on the end of the bed.

Sarah had vests in pastel colours with lace around the top. Lindsey marvelled at their daintiness compared to her own thick white ones. Anyway, she rolled them into tight cylinders. She did the same with Sarah's cropped T-shirts, the ones that exposed her tanned midriff.

Sarah's knickers and bras were flimsy and useless. But then bras were always useless. Lindsey only had one, an AA cup in plain white cotton, but she never wore it because it felt like being bandaged.

Lindsey set to work balling Sarah's socks. She tried to ball the silken pyjamas too, but they ran through her hands like cream.

The stuffed figure took up most of the room in her narrow

bed. Lindsey wondered which side she should get in. When her father was alive, he'd always slept on the right of her mother. So she pushed the figure across to the right side of the bed, went to the light switch, groped her way back to the bed in the pitch darkness and got in.

The next morning, the sight of Christ's outline told Lindsey it was about seven o'clock. Mme would be in the kitchen, boiling the kettle, opening packets of toasts, spooning green jam into a saucer. She glanced across at the other bed, expecting it still to be empty. But she saw the familiar shape of Sarah under the covers.

Suddenly wide awake, she stared at the stuffed man next to her. In the thin light of morning, the whole Pierre thing seemed ridiculous; her reaction pure lunacy. She must get the figure dismantled before Sarah woke. She began to tug down his trousers. The bedsprings twanged.

'What time is it?' Sarah asked from under her coverlet.

'Early. Go back to sleep.'

'Stop crashing about then.'

Lindsey started undoing his shirt buttons.

'What are you doing?' said Sarah.

'Nothing,' said Lindsey.

She must have drifted back to sleep because she snapped awake to what she thought was the alarm.

But it wasn't. It was Sarah sitting up in bed and screaming her head off. She was staring at the stuffed man, who had fallen out of bed and was lying face up on the floor, in the same pose as the crucified Christ.

The girls sat opposite each other on the train journey home, not talking. Sarah had insisted on facing the engine. Lindsey watched French cows and telegraph poles reel away from her, quickly in the foreground and slowly in the background, as if they were travelling on the rim of a great wheel. She imagined the black dog running next to the track, barking its thrilling, hysterical bark.

Madame had sent them packing.

Pierre had said, 'What is all ze fuss? Two silly English girls 'ave committed a small imbecility. Nussing has really 'appened.' He had given them the option of finishing their stay elsewhere. But Sarah had glared at him and said she'd rather die than stay another second in this steaming cesspool of a country. Lindsey, much to her own surprise, had said she felt the same.

Now the train was whistling through a station. Lindsey tore a piece off an *Asterix the Gaul* page and wrote her phone number on it.

Sarah curled her lip. 'What's that? I suppose you think I'm going to give you mine.'

'It would be good manners in the circumstances,' said Lindsey. 'Don't you think?'

She hadn't dared to ask whether anything had actually happened between Sarah and Pierre. But even if it had, it was over now.

Sarah tucked the slip of paper into her jeans pocket. Lindsey imagined the jeans being pulled out of the washing machine tomorrow, the paper disintegrated. 'You will remember where you've put that?'

'Probably not, kid. Shock, horror. Look. There's no point giving you my number. My parents are splitting up. I don't even know where I'll be living this time next year.'

Lindsey didn't know what to say until later, when they were passing Battersea Power Station with the four chimneys at the corners that made it look like a giant upside-down table.

'You'll be alright, you know,' Lindsey said. 'After my dad died it was awful at first, then I got used to it.'

Uncertainty crossed Sarah's face and Lindsey thought for a moment that they were going to have a conversation.

Then Sarah laughed, said, 'Yeah, right,' and, clothing her face in its normal look of remote scorn, went back to looking out of the window.

The Flight Back

Jean walked up the steep white metal steps. It was midday and the handrail was hot. At the top, she took off her sunglasses and saw that the air hostess was wearing a navy skirt and hat, stockings, court shoes, white gloves. England was arriving too soon. She went to step through the door, but must have caught her foot because a hand gripped her arm.

'Is everything alright, miss?' The lipstick smile was gone.

'Yes,' said Jean. 'I'm sorry. The light... my glasses.'

It was cool inside the plane, almost chill.

'You've mislaid your boarding pass?'

'No, I have it here.' Jean fumbled it out of her bag.

The air hostess seemed reluctant to let her go. But a queue was forming and Jean was released into the aisle, to search for seat 15a, steadying herself on the seatbacks.

She fastened her seatbelt and plucked the in-flight magazine from the pocket in front. It explained how to put on a lifejacket. All BOAC jets, it told her, flew on Castrol. A man smoked a Peter Stuyvesant cigarette; another wore a dressing gown in Viyella. A route map of the world, covered in black scribble, swam in front of her eyes. A man in a business suit sat down in the next-but-one seat. He nodded to her then drew papers from a briefcase.

To Jean's alarm, everyone ignored the airhostesses' safety demonstration. The plane hurtled down the runway and she clutched the reinforced paper bag on her lap, remembering all the glasses of palm wine she'd swallowed at the lunch the school had put on to mark her leaving. Below, the green-striped yam fields turned to postage stamps; were swallowed by cloud.

She must have dozed because she woke to a stiff neck and a tray with stew and a roll. She couldn't imagine eating, and pushed the glossy chunks around with her fork until coffee arrived and was poured, black treacle in a white cup. A headache lurked off stage; she ordered a double whisky to stave it off, and resolved not to sleep again. The airhostess from earlier on served her, tight around the mouth, and she wanted to say she didn't usually drink like this; didn't usually drink at all.

Through gaps in the cloud, she saw the veins of dried rivers below, a pillar of smoke reaching up from blackened ground. She wondered if they'd reached the Sahara yet and whether all Africa was as hot as the area where she'd lived. Some days the seed pods from the tree outside her house had exploded and rattled on the door like rifle pellets and the air had been full of dust, blocking the sun. If you went out, you got a pain at the top of your nose.

She realised that the business man was leaning across, offering her a cigarette. He was middle aged, with grey hair and bushy black eyebrows, silver-framed glasses.

She shook her head.

'You don't smoke?' he asked.

His accent was American. She'd met Americans in Nigeria, from the Peace Corps. Their first names had been like surnames: Wesley, Brent, Franklin. After a few meetings, she and the other English volunteers had drifted away from them, for no reason you could put your finger on except perhaps their confidence.

But the man had asked her a question. It was rude not to answer. 'I do smoke, actually.'

He jabbed the pack at her, a brand she didn't recognise. 'Go on. You look like you could use one.'

Black hairs sprouted from his cuff, held by cufflinks. She tried to see whether they were Playboy bunnies. If they were, she would ask to transfer to a different seat.

'Look, I've a daughter your age,' he said. 'Early twenties, am I right?'

It couldn't hurt to agree.

'So rest assured, miss, this is not a chat up. It really is just a cigarette. Hey, isn't that what Freud once said? Sometimes a cigar is just a cigar?'

She had to smile at that. She took the cigarette. When he produced his lighter, she saw that his ring finger bore a gold band and not the pale strip of skin smudged over with fake tan that her father had once warned her about.

At the Girls' Secondary, which was a boarding school, everyone had longed for letters from home. The post arrived at the school office, usually on a Friday, and the five white women would hurry across the quadrangle slitting the thin blue paper with the letter openers they kept in their handbags. They would stop under the shade of the big frangipani to gobble the main news then run to their classrooms, looking forward to later, to reading and rereading.

She'd only been there a month when her father's letter had come with the news, as if he'd been waiting for her to fly three thousand miles away before he told her. He could write beautifully; was proud of it, but on this occasion he was reduced to stock phrases. 'Your mother', he said, 'On the rocks', and 'parting of the ways'. She stood rubbing the tops of her arms and staring into space. She didn't see her girls, smart in their pristine uniforms, waving and calling. In the classroom, she forgot which la Fontaine fable they were studying.

After school, the girls, guessing something was wrong, wouldn't leave her alone. They banged on her door in the teacher's compound. They produced their new handbags and wanted their photographs taken sitting astride her moped. They demanded to do her hair. When she agreed, they cheered and clapped and then sat on her front porch singing while one of them backcombed her hair into a beehive and tied it with her own white hair-band. They fetched the mirror and Jean, soothed by the tickling of the comb, had to laugh and agree that yes, it suited her.

She didn't get back to the letter till midnight. Then, no matter how many times she reread it, the news remained the same.

The man, who was called Lloyd, was a conversationalist of the sort Jean liked; one who didn't need much encouragement to talk. He worked for the US embassy; was going to London for a meeting. He bought her another whisky; bought himself a ginger ale. She sank into the cocoon of the second drink, enjoying the cool smoke of the mentholated cigarettes, listening to his stories.

She listened while the plane stopped to refuel in Tunisia; listened again when they'd taken off and regained their altitude above the carpet of white cloud that looked solid enough to walk on.

He told her how he'd sheltered yesterday at a street vendor's stall in a downpour and had taken out his cigarettes only to have the vendor snatch them and share them out among all the people under the shelter.

'That showed me,' he said. 'World politics played out under an umbrella.' Jean smiled. She noticed that his watch looked expensive, his linen suit well cut. She thought he was probably a high up. He caught her looking, and his eyes crinkled at the edges. 'So what's a sharp cookie like you doing on a plane coming from such a – excuse me – god-forsaken hole in Africa?'

'It's hardly god-forsaken,' said Jean. 'I met more nuns and missionaries out there than you could shake a stick at.'

'Okay,' said Lloyd, 'what's a sharp cookie like you doing on a plane coming from such a religious hotbed, such an omphalos, such a bull's eye of Christianity?'

She laughed. Against the roar of the engines that she'd almost stopped noticing, she told him about her two years there; about her girls, taking and passing their French 'A' Levels last summer, the first girls in the country to do so. She talked especially about her scholarship girl, Grace. Grace's family was poor, she said, but both daughters went to school. Grace supported them by frying waste fat at the market. 'I was so proud of her,' she said. 'You can't imagine.'

Lloyd said he was sure he couldn't, though in another way he possibly could. The air hostesses moved up the aisle. Lloyd bought more whisky; more ginger ale; more Consulate cigarettes from the duty-free trolley.

In the evenings, the girls had loved to dance barefoot in traditional dress and fringed anklets to the sound of drums. Or in sling-backs and fifties' swing skirts to the sound of Frank and Nancy Sinatra; it didn't matter. She told him all about it. She told him she'd had a wrapper made out of bright local cotton;

had danced with them.

She talked until the pilot announced that he was beginning his descent and would appreciate it if passengers could extinguish their cigarettes and fasten their seat belts.

'Sorry,' she said. 'I've bored you to death. And we've smoked for England.'

'And for the US,' said Lloyd, opening the flap on the shared ashtray. 'It's been real good to meet you. I gotta tell you, my daughter Trish – she's one helluva girl in her own way – but she would never have the balls – excuse me – guts, to do what you've done. You say you're proud of your students. But your Pa must be real proud of you.'

Jean looked down; fiddled with her seatbelt. A lump had come to her throat.

She felt Lloyd's eyes on her.

'Yes,' she said. 'He is.'

On the tarmac she was grateful for the fresh air, damp and dark though it was; felt reluctant to enter the airport building, with its escalators and corridors. At passport control, she and Lloyd parted company. 'So long,' he said. 'See you again some-day on some other plane, headed for some other, excuse me, shit hole in the middle of Africa.'

'I do hope so,' she said. His handshake was firm, his smile warm. He had the gift of making other people feel at their ease. As they joined their respective queues, one long and quick, the other short and slow, she wondered again who he was. Then she gave up her passport at the booth; heard the thud as the British rubber stamp came down next to the green and purple entry and exit stamps of the other country. She was back.

She hadn't reckoned on so much concrete. It was everywhere. Roundabout after roundabout made the coach lumber nonsensically in circles. On smooth wide roads, more traffic than she had ever seen flew in one direction. Roads rose to pass over other roads; swept in long curves above trees and buildings. You could surely never cross these roads on foot; you would be crushed under a hundred wheels. There were no people, though pale faces peered from the dark interiors of cars. It was like science fiction. Jean clutched her handbag. This London was not the one she'd left.

The woman, apparently, was called Pauline. Jean thought now of other Paulines – one at primary school, who'd been fat with an even fatter brother, and whose parents had owned a sweet shop. Jean had avoided that Pauline in case unpopularity rubbed off. Then there was the young artist Pauline who stared at you from all the front pages these days, even in Nigeria, with her straw boater, freckles and black-rimmed eyes.

Her father hadn't described his Pauline; only said she was quite, quite different to Jean's mother. What had he meant? That she was a cool blonde in a fox fur? Or that she was kind and gentle and didn't make his life a misery? Jean wished she'd asked questions when she finally wrote back instead of saying that his news had come as rather a surprise and that since the rainy season had begun, it was very humid in Nigeria.

The airline magazine was rolled in her bag, a souvenir. She tried to read an article, something about the aeroplane's tail assembly, but bars of yellow light chased each other across the page and made her nauseous. She stared at an ad, an air hostess curled up on a bar stool. 'Think of her as your mother' said the heading, but the woman's miniskirt and moody stare were anything but motherly. Jean gave up on the magazine and sat with her headache and raging thirst in the dim thrum of the coach.

It was eight o'clock and very dark when she arrived at a broad wooden door in Bayswater with a panel of silver buttons beside it. It was cold and she had no coat. At Victoria, the ocean of faces had made her small, then the Underground, where people's lack of eye contact had made her invisible. A couple passed, holding hands; the woman laughed. They were in a bubble of warmth, with their scarves and gloves; their love.

She put her grip down and checked the address again. Like a fast train passing through a dark station, the alternatives shot through her mind – a room in a hostel, the family home in Whitstable, where her mother still lived. But she pressed the bell.

She was half hoping he'd forgotten, gone out, but a buzzer sounded right away. The heavy door opened with a click. She stepped into a lit lobby with a black and white tiled floor. She smelt polish; saw a chandelier. In front of her, stairs rose. She walked to the bottom. At the top of the stairwell, two heads were silhouetted.

She couldn't see her father's features; didn't need to. And the other person must be Pauline, the woman who throughout her childhood she'd never met or guessed at, the woman who for twenty-one years it seemed he'd been travelling to London to visit. She shaded her eyes against the overhead light, trying to see Pauline's face. All she could see was the hair, piled in a beehive, tied with a pale band. All she could see was a hand that shot up in greeting then fell back, as if from lack of confidence.

She stood, unable to speak or move.

It was Pauline who broke the spell, her voice small and soft. 'Jean, love. Come on up.'

Jean nodded; picked up her grip and began to make her way up the long flight of stairs.

The Common Cold

Now you were living in Nigeria, you thought that having a cold was more like having a hot. Your sneezes were dry, your head a radiator. The only cool was your mother's hand, withdrawn too soon with the announcement that yes, you were definitely well enough to go to school.

Your mother wore red lipstick and a green dress. Her winged spectacles hung on a chain around her neck.

'If you come to school, I can keep an eye on you,' she said. It was only two months since Nana had died, but she'd said that sitting around moping was doing her no good. Next thing you knew, she was an English teacher.

'Chidike could look after me here,' you said, speaking through your nose to sound as poorly as possible. You imagined games of Snap together and pushing shiny rows of ballbearings along the grooves on the iroko tabletop.

Your mother stood up. 'Chidike has work to do,' she said.

At school, the words to 'We Plough the Fields and Scatter' buzzed in your nose. When it came to the twelve times table, your brain was gone, sucked out with a straw as if South Americans were getting ready to shrink your head.

You were in the top tier. Sister Benedict taught you on Fridays. Since she'd had what your mother called a meltdown, she'd been promoted.

'Should you not be at home in your bed?' she asked. Her eyes were kinder than they used to be. It made the sadness inside you well up and you couldn't speak. 'Though of course your mammy can care for you better here. I expect that's what she was thinking.'

Morning break came but all the care you got from your mother was a frown. 'Have you been keeping cool the way I told you? And taking in plenty of water? Do you really think you'll be well enough to go to Omo's at lunchtime?'

'Yes,' you said, trying to look much, much better. Going to Omo's was always what you did on Fridays now, and Mrs Ojukwu always made a fuss of you, hugging you till your bones nearly broke and cooking you jollof rice and puff-puff.

At lunchtime, you went to the outside tap, soaked the edge of your dress in cold water and held it to the back of your neck. It made you shiver but when your mother put her hand on your forehead, she nodded and said at least you weren't any worse. You promised you would tell Mrs Ojukwu if you felt feverish.

On the Ikot Ekpene road, the brightness made you dizzy.

'Look where you are going,' said Omo, trudging beside you. She was in a bad mood. 'You will fall into the ditch.'

'Have you got beriberi?' she asked when you didn't answer.

Normally you would have pretended to be contagious and chased her but today that was beyond you. She delivered a few more taunts then fell silent.

You tramped along the side of the baking road. You came to the shrine with the Action Man and thought he must be hot in his boots and khaki uniform.

When you reached the track that led to Omo's house, she walked past.

'Where are you going?' you asked. You had already decided you couldn't walk one step further than you had to.

For once, Omo answered you straight. 'We're going to my grandmother's.'

'Why?'

'Because we are.'

'How far is it?'

'A hundred and one miles.'

'I'm going back then,' you said.

'You are not,' said Omo.

You felt as if you might fall over.

'It's not that far,' said Omo. 'Honest injun.'

It sounded like a fib, and you dragged your feet. But Omo turned down the very next track and began heading towards a group of round huts. They had roofs like shaggy hair do's.

You brightened. You'd seen lots of mud huts but had never been allowed inside one.

'Does she live in one of these?' you asked. You thought it might be a bit like Nana's outside toilet, which was being knocked down, so your mother said, by the new owners.

'Yes. But so what?' said Omo. 'She is a traditional lady.'

You didn't know what that meant. 'Is she your mother's mother?'

'How should I know?' said Omo.

At the huts, there was no-one around. Mottled pigs snored in the shade. Omo led you to a hut that looked twice as big as all the others. A few steps from the door she hissed, 'She isn't anybody's mother.'

'How can she be your grandmother, then?' you asked.

'Because she is very, very old,' said Omo.

The being who came to the doorway did indeed look so old

that you thought, since the rules for grandmothers were different out here, that she might be a man. Then you saw the flattened bosoms, wrinkled as Christmas dates, that lay on her chest. You tried not to look at them again. Her hair was grey wisps. You couldn't describe her eyes. When she looked at you, you stayed looked at. You had never seen anyone so old.

In the hut, which had no windows, she showed you to a row of raffia mats. You were glad to sit; would have liked to lie.

She turned to Omo. As they talked, in their own language, she glanced at you as if she thought you could understand. You smiled, to be polite, but after a while you gave up, because she didn't smile back. She didn't smile at Omo either, or kiss her or throw her hands up, or do anything else grandmothers were supposed to do.

Eventually she went to the back of the hut, got three bowls and started filling them from a black pot.

'What were you talking about?' you whispered.

'It does not matter,' said Omo. She was sitting up straight on her mat. She wasn't her normal slouching self. Her eyes flicked to the old woman.

'You weren't talking about *me*, were you?' It was meant to be a joke, but when Omo didn't reply you knew you had accidentally hit on the truth. Nervous wings fluttered in your chest. 'What were you saying?'

Omo's eyes flicked to her grandmother again. It was as if she was a big spider whose movements had to be constantly monitored.

'She said you were sick,' she whispered.

'With my cold?'

'Shut your mouth,' said Omo. 'She will hear you.'

And then you understood: Omo was frightened of her grandmother. It made you want to laugh. You thought of Nana with her white fluffy hair, her hatpins and brooches that she kept pinned to a piece of brown velvet and her big leg that had to be bandaged. No-one could ever be frightened of her.

The three of you sat on the mats to eat your rice. You'd never seen an old person on the floor before. If Nana knelt on her weeding stool among the pansies and snapdragons, she said it took her half an hour to get up again.

'Silence while eating is a rule of grandmothers when children are present,' Omo said, as if she was reciting lines in school assembly. 'It is to prevent them choking.'

You were riveted by the sight of Omo obeying rules.

While you ate, silent, you spotted a row of clay pots in the darkness at the back of the hut. They had spouts and handles like normal pots, but they were covered in lumps. The lumps, you realised as you went on looking, were bosoms, and heads with blind eyes. And babies. Some of the pots had useless-looking arms, not just one set, but two. As for the spouts, you now saw that they were shaped like mouths, and the handles like noses.

You thought of the high shelf that went all round your Aunt Gladys' sitting room in Cheltenham and from which a hundred red cheeked little jug-men looked down, fat and shiny.

Omo always ate fast but today she seemed to be in a race. Soon her bowl was empty. 'We must go,' she whispered.

But you were fascinated by the pots. It was like the things Joseph Adeola brought to school in matchboxes. You didn't want to look at them but they put a juju on your eyes so that you had to. You edged closer. 'What are those pots for?'

Omo glanced at her relative, who was still eating. 'Grandmother is a potter. Now she is old, she is allowed to make any kind of pot she likes. Finish your food.'

'What do you mean, allowed?'

'She made forbidden pots when she was young. That is what made her barren,' Omo whispered.

You looked at the grandmother. It seemed rude to speak about her like that. But she went on slowly pinching up rice and putting it into her mouth. Perhaps she didn't speak English.

You wondered what forbidden pots were and whether these were they. 'What does she do with them?' you asked.

'Let's get out of here,' said Omo.

You almost laughed. Normally you were the scared one, not Omo. 'In a minute,' you said.

Then you sneezed and sneezed again and it made your throat hurt so much that you groaned.

The grandmother looked at you with her sharp eyes and said something to Omo.

'*Na, na,*' said Omo. '*Biko, biko.*'

'What did she say?' you asked.

'She wants to cure you of your sickness,' said Omo. Her voice was quiet.

'There's no cure for the common cold, everyone knows that,' you said.

'She says she will make you a pot to cure it.'

'How's that going to help?'

But the old woman stood up and beckoned you to the place in the hut where it was dimmest of all. '*Mbeke, mbeke,*' she said. It would have been very rude not to obey her, so you got up and went to the back of the hut.

207

Omo put her hands over her eyes. 'Mary Mother of God,' she said.

At the back of the hut, the grandmother pressed you down onto some sacking. The row of pots looked on. She called you Mbeke again, even though Omo had introduced you as Sarah. Perhaps your real name was hard for her to say.

Then she went out of the huts. She came back in with two big wet handfuls of mud, the water from it running through her fingers; standing like beads on the dirt floor. Crouching beside you, she kneaded and stretched it.

Omo said afterwards that, being your best friend, she never took her eyes off you for a second in case grandmother turned you into a yam beetle. But now, from the depths of the hut, all you could see when you looked for Omo was light. You thought she'd gone; were afraid to ask.

The mud was cool and heavy on your face and neck and you shivered. You tasted rice in your mouth and hoped you wouldn't be sick. The grandmother pressed more mud to your nose and mouth. You thought she was going to suffocate you but at the last moment she made air holes.

The mud was plastered all over your ears now, and down the left side of your chest, on top of your school blouse. You had no idea how you were going to explain that to your mother.

The normal world went far away. Time passed. Smells drifted to your nostrils; of greenery, then burning, then something sharp and bitter. The mask pinned you down, made you forget you had ever been able to move. You felt like a monitor lizard.

You might have dozed because when the weight was lifted from your face you were startled; the light was extra bright, and someone was pulling at your hands.

It was Omo. 'Come *on*. It is time for us to go home now.'

She sounded cross. She sounded like her normal self and before you even sat up and looked around, you knew that the hut was empty of Grandmother. 'Where is she?'

'She has finished. It is alright, she told me we could go.'

As you stood up, you did an experimental swallow but your throat still hurt a lot, as if someone had sandpapered it down the back. Your nose was blocked solid. You eyed the inside-out clay mask that Omo had lifted from your face.

'I'm not any better,' you said.

Omo looked at you. 'Grandmother says you will be.'

You didn't know what you'd been expecting, but when Omo brought the pot to school on Monday morning, it was small and round with lots of tiny spouts, like beaks.

'Grandmother says we are lucky it is the dry season,' said Omo. 'She cannot make these pots when it rains.'

'Why not?' you asked.

Omo shrugged.

'That pot is creepy,' you said.

'You have to keep it in your bedroom,' said Omo. 'Normally you would have to fire your own pot, but grandmother did it for you.'

'What's firing?' you asked.

'Who cares?' said Omo. 'What is important is that you have got to keep this pot safe. You are healed, but if you break the pot, the sickness will come back.'

You took the pot from her. It was heavy and cool. You made yourself touch the sharp beaks. They were the only openings to the dark inside.

'What happens if I knock one of the beaks off?' you asked. 'By accident, I mean. Do I still get ill? Or are accidents allowed?'

'You will get a severe headache,' said Omo. But you could tell she'd made it up.

'Anyway I'm *not* healed,' you said. If anything, your cold was worse, with a cough that shook you till your eyes watered.

'I'm only telling you what she said,' said Omo.

'Do you believe her?' you asked. Omo didn't reply.

You thought about the house in Fuel Plantation. You thought about your wardrobe and the space under your bed. You wondered if there was anywhere in the whole world you could hide the pot where your mother wouldn't immediately find it. You decided there wasn't.

At home after lunch you went to find Chidike. He was at the bottom of the compound near the servants' hut. He was wearing his red check shirt, which meant he was still on duty. The cicadas chirped from the golf course.

He stepped back when you took the pot out of your dress pocket. '*Chei!* What is this?'

'It's a pot,' you said. 'I've got to not break it, whatever happens.'

Chidike sucked air in through his teeth. 'What you want *me* go do with it?'

'Keep it safe for me. Please,' you said, eyeing the concrete block with its bead curtain and its mesh windows; the two rooms that your mother never entered.

Chidike was the kindest person you knew, except for Nana, and Omo's mother. But he shook his head. 'Your fadder know you bring juju into the house?'

You frowned. 'It's not juju,' you said, even though you thought it probably was. 'It's a pot.'

Chidike looked stern. 'Na, na.'

You longed for Nana. She knew all about magic; tealeaves and such. Black cats and four-leaved clovers. She wouldn't have been frightened. You sighed and put the pot back in your pocket, hating being alone with a secret you hadn't asked for in the first place.

'Alright,' you said. 'Sorry to bother you.'

Chidike's voice startled you. 'Okay,' he said. 'I will take this ugly thing. I will put it in a dark corner, where I cannot see it.'

He was smiling, and when he took the pot, you didn't know whether he'd suddenly changed his mind or whether he'd been teasing you from the start. You threw your arms around him, anyway.

That night you had a dream, one you would still remember forty years later. Nana was alive and you walked with her, hand-in-hand, through an English meadow. The sun shone; wildflowers swayed on their stalks. But you knew you had to hurry. Nana dawdled; wouldn't take you seriously. You glanced behind but you couldn't quite see what was following you. You tugged at her hand and pleaded, but she wouldn't change her pace. And her pace was too slow, you knew.

You woke in the dark, screaming and beating at the mosquito net. When the door opened, it was your mother, wearing her long white nightie.

You thought she would be cross with you for waking your father up. But she came and sat on the edge of your bed, took you in her arms and stroked your head and said there, there, darling, don't cry. When you clung to her, for once she didn't try and prise your fingers loose. She said she knew it was a sad time and that you'd had a bad dream but that the fear would pass. She said lots of things. Her voice was wobbly, as though she was nearly crying herself. But she said everything was going to be alright and she said it with such certainty that you believed her.

Mandy Sutter went to school in Nigeria and Bromley but now lives in Yorkshire with her partner and a large black dog called Fable. She writes a popular blog, The Reluctant Gardener. She has cowritten two nonfiction books about Somali women. Her first novel, *Stretching It*, was published in 2013, her third poetry pamphlet, *Old Blue Car*, in 2015. She won first prize in the New Welsh Writing Awards in 2016 for the chapter 'Bush Meat'.

Acknowledgements and Thanks

'Munachi Bones' was published in *Mslexia*, issue 65, 2015

A version of 'Seed' was published in *Ambit*, issue 222, 2015 and in *End Notes*, Edge Publishing, 2017

A version of 'The Sea Spirit' was published in *Are You She*, Tindal Street Press, 2004

Heartfelt thanks to: Ted Bassett, Sarah Ward, Nicolas Hawkes and Sarah Connell for telling me your spellbinding stories. To Jim Hinks and my novel group (you know who you are) for your support years back: it meant a lot. To Hilary Mantel, Penelope Shuttle, Lesley Glaister, Alison Moore, Kath McKay, Ray French and Rory MacLean for championing my stories along the way and to my editor Gwen Davies for her perceptiveness and for making it all happen in such a lovely way.

Reviews of Mandy Sutter's Writing

'Atmospheric... wonderfully unexpected... disquieting, touching and darkly humorous.'

Alison Moore, author of Booker-shortlisted *The Lighthouse*

'Triumphs, in its lean prose and true dialogue... disarming humour... [and] evocation of a family divided by sexism and racism in 1960s Nigeria. Sutter stitches together the threads of memory to create a moving tapestry of lost life, building bridges of understanding across time and place, enhancing literature's ever-changing, ever-supple genre.'

Rory MacLean, NWWA 2016 co-judge & author of *Berlin: Imagine a City*

'Mandy Sutter's Nigeria rises like a mirage... [creating] a complete arc of innovative concision.'

Gwen Davies, NWWA 20016 co-judge

'[The chapter "The Sea Spirit"] demonstrates... the power of story.... [capturing] something of the magic and bewilderment of a child's perceptions yet allows a "glimmer of fear, a shiny edge" to glint through.'

Lesley Glaister

>>

'In [the chapter] "Munachi Bones", Sutter depicts the sidelining and silencing of older ways of life in an African village. We discern, in a microcosm, what has happened and is happening in macrocosm in much of the developing world. The [section] uses powerful dialogue and the characters spring to life with immediacy, attesting to this writer's accuracy both of ear and eye. The strange names given to people... are witty and apt, reminding us that there is a particular art in naming. The prose style is clean, full of impact, fast-paced, balancing the story at the cusp of past and present. The evocation of village sounds and smells is wonderful – I love the market especially – and there is a deep understanding both of human wisdom and un-wisdom.'

Penelope Shuttle

'There's a laconic relish about Sutter's best work that makes it always readable.'

John Lucas, *Stand*

'Sutter's observation of human foibles and the complexity of both romantic and family relationships is spot on.'

Yvette Huddleston, *Yorkshire Post*

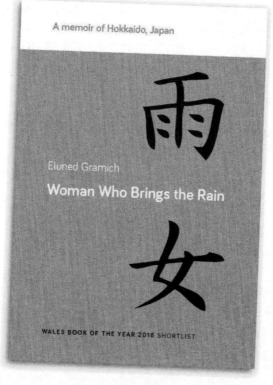